Rhombus - Text copyright © Emmy Ellis 2024
Cover Art by Emmy Ellis @ studioenp.com © 2024

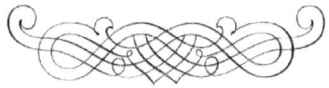

All Rights Reserved

Rhombus is a work of fiction. All characters, places, and events are from the author's imagination. Any resemblance to persons, living or dead, events or places is purely coincidental.

The author respectfully recognises the use of any and all trademarks.

With the exception of quotes used in reviews, this book may not be reproduced or used in whole or in part by any means existing without written permission from the author.

Warning: The unauthorised reproduction or distribution of this copyrighted work is illegal. No part of this book may be scanned, uploaded, or distributed via the Internet or any other means, electronic or print, without the author's written permission.

RHOMBUS

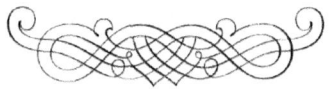

Emmy Ellis

Chapter One

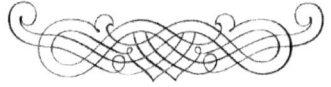

In the cold chill of a January evening, Hailey Parr ran down the street towards town. She shivered at the memory of what had just happened. It appeared in her mind's eye, each frame a violent staccato flash. Leaving Delaney overnight at Mum's so he was safe. Joe coming home to find her packing. His fury. She'd

never believed people's eyes could turn black in a rage until then, but his had. So, so black.

She knew damn well why she was off to buy a new quilt for Delaney's bed, but why did the insistent urge that she do it tonight push her along the street? While his current one only had a little blood on it, easily spot-washed, she had the uncontrollable need to replace it right away. Dump the old one. Maybe that blood would be too much to look at if she cleaned it. Or maybe, because such violence had occurred in her son's bedroom, she needed to make sure she eradicated all traces of it, at least from her home. But it would always be in her mind. Blood was never really gone anyway, even if it looked like it was. Was it the same for sperm?

She retched at that, how it was sticky between her legs.

The side of her wrist stung from the knife slashes. After he'd…after he'd done what no man should, he'd stormed out, and with her knickers and leggings still around her ankles, bunched against her trainers, she'd stood at Delaney's window and checked which way Joe had gone. Off towards Kitchen Street to the women he likely fucked as well as persuading them to buy drugs off his scutty little runners. Or was there more to him being in that street? Yes, there was, but she couldn't contemplate it at the minute.

Finding out about Kitchen Street was why she'd packed to go away for a few days to her aunt's house in Wales. Take Delaney and hide while The Brothers sorted Joe—because she planned to tell them everything, let them deal with him. What she'd found out…no, she didn't want any part of it.

She'd waited a few seconds, getting herself presentable and shrugging on her coat, stuffing her phone in her handbag, then left her house, going in the opposite direction to him. This was insane, what she was doing. A new quilt wouldn't fix anything, and neither would the police, unfortunately. They couldn't. In the past, she'd rung them about Joe from a phone in the Red Lion, although admittedly she hadn't given her name or his. Too scared to. She'd told them about his threats towards her, just so someone knew and she wasn't bottling it up inside, but without her revealing her identity, they were powerless to act.

She rushed past the top end of the street where The Angel stood, fighting the urge to go inside and drink a vodka to steady her nerves. Working women stood on the corner, reminding her of Joe and how he apparently prowled, and she continued on, making it to the road where all the shops were. People, humanity, safety. Life going on as normal, as if she hadn't just been used and abused by a man who'd said he loved her.

Lies, everything he said was lies.

A few places were still open, so she entered Home Bargains, heading for the bedding section. A blonde woman stood in front of the king-size quilt covers, a roll of black rubbish bags and some tumble dryer sheets in her pull-along basket. Oh God, it was Joe's ex. Stacey.

Of all the people to bump into.

Hailey moved past her to the single duvets and stretched her hand out to grab a fifteen tog.

"Oh fuck, no," Stacey said. "No."

Hailey froze. Stacey stared at the knife slashes, the crude J cut into the side of Hailey's wrist inside a rhombus, smothered in scuffed blood where her coat sleeve had brushed against it, fresh scarlet still rising into the cuts. Hailey held the duvet to her chest, backing away, tugging her sleeve down to hide her humiliation.

"Joe Osbourne?" Stacey pulled her jacket sleeve up, showing a tattoo. "My scar's under that."

Hailey stopped reversing. "I have to go… He'll…"

"Wait!" Stacey advanced, dragging her basket behind her. "This can't be allowed to happen again. Can we go for a chat? Please? I'm Stacey. I used to go out with Joe."

"I know who you are."

Stacey paused, perhaps reading Hailey's expression. "I know what he's like, love. I know."

Why did I come here? Why did I have to see her?

Hailey had heard all sorts of things about Joe's ex. He'd slagged her off umpteen times, saying she was a nagging cow and had set her brothers on him for no reason. She was a nutter, all that sort of thing. He'd likely say the same about Hailey to whoever he latched on to next, if she ever got him to leave her alone, and he maybe even said it already to those women on Kitchen Street, the likes of, "She doesn't understand me, we've grown apart." All bollocks.

Would there be any harm in this? Talking?

There will be if he finds out.

But you're telling the twins. You'll be in Wales when it all kicks off.

"Okay," Hailey blurted, desperate to tell someone other than the police on the end of a phone line.

It had been so hard, keeping it from Mum, lying to her, saying everything was all right when it fucking well wasn't. Fobbing the mothers off at the school gates, saying she'd tripped over Delaney's toys and that was why she had a bruise. Making out to Delaney that Mummy's black eye was from walking into a cupboard door while he was at school. He was only little and didn't need to know what she'd been through. She avoided Mum if she had marks on her, unless she covered them with makeup.

"*I'll just grab these, then we'll go.*" *Stacey dropped a quilt cover in her basket and opted for a thirteen-tog quilt.* "*I've got a spare room now, just doing it up.*"

Stacey smiled, perhaps knowing that for now, inane conversation was best. They were in a shop, after all, and airing dirty laundry in public, especially this *dirty laundry, wasn't something Hailey wanted to do.*

At the till, Stacey popped her things on the conveyor belt, taking Hailey's quilt off her and adding it to her purchases. "*If I know him, you can't afford that. He'll be taking your money off you.*"

Shame burned Hailey's cheeks. She'd managed to stop him doing that by hiding her spare cash, but she wasn't going to argue. If Stacey wanted to buy it, she could.

"*Been there, done that,*" *Stacey said.* "*And before you say anything, it's okay, I can get it. Not a problem, all right?*"

Hailey nodded, her eyes stinging at the kindness. She hadn't had much of that in her life lately, although to be fair, Mum was good to her. She looked after Delaney without complaint, built blanket forts with him and actually got inside to have a tea party while they watched telly on her tablet. She was a better parent than Hailey who hadn't done anything like that for months, too coiled up because of Joe to have any energy for mucking around with her son. Her mental bandwidth was taken up with what he might do or say next, how she could get away from him.

"Do you need a bag?" the girl behind the counter asked.

Hailey had zoned out, so she snapped her attention back to reality.

"Bugger, I forgot to bring any," Stacey said. "Hang on, we'll use a couple of the black bags."

Stacey sorted that, paid, and led the way out of the shop. She handed Hailey the black bag containing Delaney's quilt and glanced up and down the street. "Shall we go in that café over the road?"

Hailey shook her head. "No, he might see us. Or someone he knows might."

Stacey nodded. "Sorry, I forgot how much you have to be careful. That or my mind's blanked it out. All right, what about Lil's Laundrette? I was going there after Home Bargains anyway to wash this quilt. He… I'd bought a new one before, and that night, he… Well, let's just say the new-quilt smell reminds me of it. Tends to when your face is pushed into it."

Hailey nodded. Christ, Joe was such a wanker. He was apparently a serial rapist now as well.

Stacey looked around them again. "Listen, do you need me to walk on until we've left town so we're not seen here together?"

"Yes."

Stacey strutted off, and Hailey waited a moment or two, then followed. At the end of the street, they turned a corner into a residential area. It was risky being here, because they headed towards the Noodle and Tiger, which was on the way to Lil's. Joe could be near there, checking on his runners.

Hailey put her head down, nerves spiking.

Stacey sighed. "So you've been through the love-bombing, manipulation, the gaslighting, the threats. The next stage, after he puts a J and that diamond on your wrist, is rape, and after that, slicing you down below." She'd said it nonchalantly, and maybe that was because giving it any real thought brought back too many horrific memories.

Hailey gasped, a sharp breath in, but she didn't lift her head. Joe had said something similar to her earlier. "He raped me. Tonight. He's never done that before."

"Bastard. My brothers, they got hold of him after he'd cut me. Beat the shit out of him. Maybe I should have gone to the actual Brothers, you know, got them

to deal with him. He wouldn't have dared hurt you, then. I feel so guilty that we didn't completely stop him. I should have done more. I—"

"Don't." Hailey could imagine how Stacey must have felt, her sole focus getting away from Joe, just needing it all to fuck off so she could move on and try to forget him. "I take it you didn't go to the police."

"There would have been no point. Joe's got one of them in his pocket—were you aware of that? It would have been swept under the carpet. You can just see it—woman claims boyfriend raped her, so how can that be proved when they usually had sex anyway? Honestly, I just wanted him to bog off and leave me alone. He did because of my brothers. I've often wished I'd asked them to kill him, though. Made it look like an accident or something."

Hailey had thought that as he'd grunted behind her, holding her hands above her head in one hand so she couldn't scratch him, his other on the back of her head, her cheeks and nose mashed into Delaney's quilt, his thrusts so violent. She'd wished Joe dead, thinking of all the ways she could do it, just so she didn't have to face what he'd been doing.

"You ever think about leaving again, and I'll slice your fucking cunt…"

It was ridiculous that she'd even had to think about leaving her own home. It wasn't Joe's, he just treated it like his whenever he deigned to visit. He didn't go there that often anymore, which was why she'd been poking around, asking questions, convinced he had another woman. She'd have used that as an excuse to end things with him. Then she'd found out about him running the county drug line, using sex workers, and she'd hatched her plan.

Some plan. It hadn't worked out too well, had it. Just her luck that on the evening she'd packed a case, he'd turned up. Caught her.

If only she hadn't given him a key…

"Where the fuck do you think *you're* going, bitch?"

A shiver trickled up her spine just thinking about it.

"Taking Delaney on holiday."

"Without telling me? You bastard whore! You've got another bloke, haven't you? Running off for a dirty weekend."

She'd been in Delaney's room, adding some of his clothes to the case on the floor.

"You belong to me, don't forget that."

He'd produced a flick-knife from his pocket, grabbing her arm and pinning it to the wall beside a

Minecraft poster. Their sides against the wall, his back to her front, he'd carved the J, the rhombus, the pain so evil.

"Me, too," she said to Stacey, all the anger at him resurfacing—*yes, she wanted to kill him for what he'd done.*

Who the fuck did he think he was? How **dare** *he cut her in her son's bedroom, or anywhere, force himself on her, then piss off as if she meant nothing, expecting her to be there the next time he bothered to come round.*

"I'd love to do it." *Saying it out loud, God, how liberating.*

"Seriously?" Stacey stopped beneath a lamppost and stared at her. "Because I'm down for that now I know he's done it to someone else. He's scum."

"What?"

"If we plan it right..." Stacey sighed. "I can see you didn't mean it. Forget I said anything." She continued walking.

Hailey trotted to catch up, her palm sweating against the black bag. "I did mean it."

They crossed the road opposite Lil's.

"Then we've got a few things to discuss. And because of what he does for a living, stabbing him is best. It'd look more plausible. Some druggie turning on him or whatever."

They stopped outside Lil's. Hailey stared inside. Lil stood behind the counter, but no one else was in there.

"Come on," Stacey said. "Let's get these quilts washed and see what we come up with between us. But you've got to promise me you'll never tell anyone what we did. I've got a good life now, and I don't want to fuck it up."

"I want a good life, so…"

They entered Lil's. Hailey hadn't been here for ages, not since before she'd saved up to buy her own secondhand washing machine. She'd had long brown hair then, in the days prior to Joe. She'd had it cut shorter, dyed it blonde for him. Did so many other things for him.

Like pretending she'd forgotten Delaney's father, Riley. But she never had. Riley had been the love of her life, her childhood sweetheart. Three years ago, he'd crossed a busy street one day, got knocked down by some prick speeding away from the police. His head injuries had been too severe for him to survive. Two years later, she'd met Joe.

Quilts in the machine, they sat with their backs to Lil. Talked quietly for a moment, Hailey cringing that Stacey had mentioned murder. Couldn't she bloody talk in code? Hailey stared at their reflection in the front window, spotting Lil sticking earbuds in and prodding at her phone, likely putting music on.

Hailey relaxed.

"He's changed his women," Stacey said. "Did you know that?"

"I found out, yes."

"He's on Kitchen Street now."

Hailey nodded. Listened to Stacey giving her the gossip as if she kept tabs on Joe, and maybe she did. Hailey asked herself if this was real or whether she'd passed out on Delaney's bed and currently dreamt. Killing Joe, it was such a big thing to do. But she wanted to feel the knife slicing into him, so he knew the pain of it, like she knew from when he'd carved her wrist.

She wanted him gone, for good. And she was at the point now where she felt she had nothing to lose. If she got caught and went to prison, Delaney would be all right with Mum, shared custody with Riley's parents. Was this what Joe had reduced her to? Someone selfish enough to expect her mother and others to give up their independence to raise their grandchild?

Or was she desperate enough?

Yes. And Hailey hated herself for that.

Chapter Two

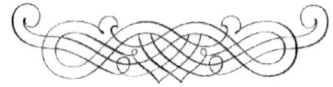

In disguise, his fake beard itching his skin, Ichabod Ahearn followed the blondes after they'd left the laundrette. Tonight, their second meeting there, had proved Lil *had* heard what she'd heard last week. The women *did* have murder in mind but hadn't said who they wanted to kill. He'd pretended to be listening to music, earbuds in, as had Lil, all planned when she'd spoken to The Brothers a few days ago.

He'd got the sense they weren't crazy bitches just out to kill someone for the sake of it. This was a move they'd been pushed into, although he reckoned one was more determined than the other. Whoever he was, he'd hurt the women badly. Had the police previously been involved in a domestic violence situation? Had the blondes thought of the consequences of killing a man who'd been aggressive towards them? That they'd perhaps become suspects? Just because they were females, didn't mean they wouldn't go to the top of the list.

The cold nipped at the tops of his cheeks, and he was glad of the casual clothing he'd opted for tonight. Trackie bottoms, a sweatshirt, the hood up. He kept to the shadows, his footsteps light. The ladies parted ways at the Noodle. The one with long hair went down the road past the pub, while the other, with a short and wispy bob, headed onwards. He could stop her, ask what she was playing at, see if she needed any help, but his instructions had been to follow one of them home. Knowing where she lived would reveal who she was with a quick database search. The twins could get their new copper, Bryan Flint, to find out, or maybe she was already on their radar and they knew her name anyway.

In the laundrette, the would-be killers had discussed tomorrow night, whether 'he' would be there, wherever 'there' was. One of them had bought the 'thing'—a knife, Ichabod presumed, seeing as Lil had reported about a stabbing on the cards the previous week. They were meeting at half seven in The Angel, then going to where 'he' was. They wanted the satisfaction of killing the man themselves as opposed to contacting George and Greg about it. Little did they know the twins would give them the option of killing. All they'd do was round the eejit up, take him to their warehouse, and the women could do the rest. Then George would saw up the body and dispose of the pieces in the Thames.

A particular part of their conversation came back to him.

"What if we get caught? There are so many cameras around these days."

"We won't. Why do you think he stands where he does of a night? He wouldn't be selling there if there was a chance he'd get nicked."

"And it's dark. Those streetlights have been broken. I walked past there today with Delaney."

"See? It'll be fine."

This was all grand. No cameras meant the twins wouldn't be seen when apprehending the man. There was no way they'd allow these two to stab someone on a street where Debbie's watchers kept an eye on the sex workers there, not to mention the bodyguard Greg had assigned to Ineke, a woman he'd taken a fancy to who worked the night shift looking after the girls. And the workers themselves, they didn't need to witness that.

It was best The Brothers took over.

The young lady ahead turned into town, a street full of shops in the middle of the residential area. All were closed bar a restaurant, a takeaway pizza place, and the Red Lion. She walked with her head down, the washing she'd done at the laundrette in a bag that bounced against her leg with each step. She glanced sideways at people walking by, as if fearful she'd bump into someone she knew. Maybe the CCTV here was giving her the willies, too. After the murder, if she was closely linked to the victim, her every move prior to it would be checked by the police. She'd have to explain, if she'd been captured on film with her sidekick, how they knew each other and why they'd been together. Bennett, a man in the twins' employ who worked the local CCTV, had already found footage of them at the laundrette last week, following their route to where they'd parted ways.

If they were both associates of the soon-to-be victim, their downfall wasn't far in the future. They had to be stopped before they got themselves arrested.

She walked past the end of the street where The Angel was located, glancing at Debbie's women on the corner. Was she thinking about the man she wanted to kill and whether he'd sampled any of them? Lil had overheard talk of him changing his women, so had he used any of this lot before?

She dipped into Princeton Avenue, the houses built directly against the pavements. Halfway down, she paused and, guessing she was about to turn around, Ichabod ducked behind a parked car. She looked the other way then, clearly watching out for 'him'. Who the feck was he? Not knowing was hampering things.

She inserted a key into number seventeen and entered. In the laundrette, she'd said her mother was looking after her sleeping son, Delaney, which would account for the lights being on. Going by the earlier conversation, this woman had lied to her mother, saying her washing machine was broken, hence why she'd gone to Lil's—which was odd, because didn't the mum have a machine she could borrow? Couldn't she have done the washing for her? Would the mother pose a problem? Was she the nosy type, well able to get information out of her daughter?

That could mess things up if she pushed and pushed until the bobbed blonde confessed to murder.

Best we get tae her before it comes tae that, then.

Chapter Three

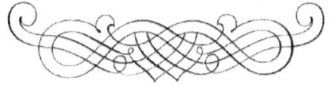

Laundrette Lil had sodded it. She'd left the laundrette, even though people were in there doing their washing. A quick, "Fuck about in here, nick anything off me, and The Brothers will be after you!" soon put her mind at rest. The fearful glances sent her way told her no one would dare try to get into her precious washing detergent cabinet and nick all her Daz and Lenor. No one wanted the twins after them, and she blessed the day she'd sold her business to them, the responsibility of running it as just a manager less stressful.

She'd followed Ichabod, determined to get in on these shenanigans. She hadn't had this much drama in ages, apart from the type she created on social media, leaving troll messages to wind people up. Although she worked in the laundrette in the evenings, by day she was an entertainer in care homes. Her being fifty-two, her dreams of becoming a star were way behind her, unless she went on *Britain's Got Talent*, so she sang karaoke to the old people and brightened their days. And hers. She hadn't exactly had the best life when it came to men—she'd killed two of the buggers—so tonight, this…well, it was all a bit thrilling, wasn't it?

In Princeton Avenue, she stood behind a Transit parked outside number twelve and peered around it. Ichabod rose from his hiding spot at the back of a car now the woman had gone indoors. Lil knew a few people down here, so it would be easy enough to find out who the soon-to-be killer was, although she'd avoid knocking on a certain woman's door. Only, she didn't think Ichabod or the twins would appreciate her butting in without asking first, so perhaps she'd better not.

Ichabod came towards her, engrossed in tapping on his phone screen. He was probably reporting back to George and Greg. Lil jumped out from behind the van, her "Boo!" putting the Irishman into a crouching ninja stance.

He twigged it was her and lowered his I'll-chop-your-throat hands. "For feck's sake, Lil, what the feckin' hell are ye *doin'*?"

"I came out for some fresh air."

He walked down the street, saying over his shoulder, "So ye just happened tae come this way, did ye? I wasn't born yesterday."

She chuckled and rushed to keep up.

His phone beeped, and he held it up to read the message. Lil peered at it, glad she'd remembered to put her glasses on tonight.

GG: WAIT AND SEE IF THE MOTHER LEAVES.

Ichabod replied with a 'yes' then stuffed his mobile in his pocket. "I take it ye nosed at that."

"Of course I fucking did. Here, pop into this alley."

Lil darted down a short passageway between houses, wheelie bins in a row along one side. Ichabod poked half his face round to watch the street, and Lil poked hers around him. They were in between streetlights, so she reckoned they were safe enough.

"Ye should go back tae the laundrette," he whispered.

"What, when all this excitement's going on?"

"What if that fella they want tae kill comes here? I don't want ye witnessin' anythin' that might upset ye."

"What if I told you I'd not only witnessed two murders but I was the one to actually commit them?"

He didn't swivel his head round to gape at her, but she'd bet he wanted to.

"Ye what?"

"That's a story for me to tell you over a drink or two. I've never admitted that to anyone before, other than Ron."

"Cardigan?"

"Hmm."

"Feckin' hell. Were ye in with him or summat?"

"Or summat. I was what he called a Treacle. Basically his woman of the moment until he got bored and found someone else."

"So he used ye."

"Yep, but I used him an' all, so fair's fair."

"Jaysus."

Lil pressed into his back. It was bloody cold, and she needed his warmth. She'd stupidly come out without collecting her coat from the staffroom, although she'd taken her handbag from beneath the counter. Her jumper did nothing to keep her warm, it wasn't thick enough.

"Shh," he said.

Lil peered ahead. Oh, fucking hell, Noelle Parr came out of number seventeen, where the blonde lived. She walked towards them in her fluffy slippers, and Ichabod pulled his head back into the passageway, Lil going with him. Both times the blondes had been in the laundrette, she hadn't seen their faces, and to be honest, even if she had, she wouldn't have recognised Noelle's daughter, not after all these years. She'd been a baby last time she'd clapped eyes on her.

Heart thumping, the bitter past lurching into Lil's mind, she leaned against the wall and waited for Noelle to go by. The *slap-slap-slap* of the slippers sounded so loud, and she scrunched her eyes shut, as if that would stop Noelle seeing her if she happened to glance down the alley. The noise receded, and Lil opened her eyes. Ichabod had turned and stared after Noelle, so, standing in front of him, Lil did the same.

Noelle entered a house farther down, just like Lil had known she would.

Lil spun round to look at Ichabod. "I need a fucking drink after that."

"Why, too much excitement for ye? I thought that's what ye wanted."

"I'll explain in the boozer."

"What about the laundrette?"

"I'll get Maria to go down and sit there until closing. Pay her overtime. Or her daughter can do it. Chelsey likes earning extra cash." She took her phone out at the same time Ichabod withdrew his from a pocket. She messaged Maria, full of apologies, lying about a sudden dicky tummy, tacking on that chilli disagreed with her.

MARIA: NO PROBLEM. CHELSEY WILL DO IT. I'M BUSY WATCHING *VERA*.

Ichabod glanced up from his phone, eyeing her funny. "Is there somethin' ye need tae tell me? If there is, ye'd better say it now."

Lil sighed out a shaky breath. "The blonde is Hailey Parr, and that was her mother, Noelle. Now come on, I need a voddy in me."

Ichabod prodded at his phone again. "That'll save the twins havin' tae get hold of their copper now I know her name. I need tae wait for their reply before I can go, though."

His phone trilled, and once again, Lil read the screen.

GG: Leave it with us. Pop back later to make sure everything's okay, then go home.

Lil smiled. "Right, so you're free to leave. Come on."

She marched off towards town, Ichabod's barely there footsteps behind her, the eerie bastard. The man was like an assassin the way he crept along, and if she didn't know he was there, she might have thought she was alone. She pushed open the door to the Red Lion and advanced on the bar so quickly she got a few filthy looks; she'd bumped her elbow into a couple of men standing there gassing and hadn't apologised.

She'd never apologise to a man ever again, even if she was in the wrong.

She ordered a double vodka for herself and a Guinness for Ichabod, then paid via Apple Wallet on her phone. A free table in the corner called to her, so she barged over there and sat. A hefty gulp of vodka soothed her nerves a little, and her guilt, which always reared up whenever she thought about Noelle. If it wasn't for Lil, that woman would still have a husband. He wouldn't be dead, disposed of by Lil and Ron Cardigan.

Ichabod sat. "What the feck's got the wind up ye?"

"If you promise to act like a priest and keep it to yourself, I'll confess."

"Will it put me in a compromisin' position wid the twins?"

"Nope, this all happened in Ron's day, nothing to do with them."

"Right, on ye go, then."

Lil prepared to get things off her ample chest. If Hailey was going through what her mother had, what Lil had, then it was no wonder she wanted to commit murder. Lil swigged more vodka then took a deep breath. Maybe telling someone all about it, someone who hadn't been involved, would finally put the memories to rest.

Chapter Four

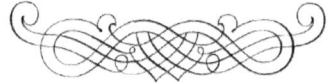

Hailey had double-locked the front door and put the chain across once Mum had left. She stared down at Delaney tucked up in his bed, grateful he hadn't woken when she'd come home. She loved him to death but could do without him needing her tonight. It was the eve of the murder, and she had far too much to think about. Delaney was a good kid, but he nattered too much, and having that in her earhole would drive her insane.

She moved to stand at the window, peering out through a chink in the curtains, worried Joe would rock up. She had no emotional energy to deal with another row, nor could she face his threats or if he wanted to have sex. The idea of *that* revolted her. How had she ever thought he was attractive? How could she have been so stupid to fall for his charms?

Because you took him at face value in the beginning and thought he was like Riley.

She forced her thoughts away from him. He didn't deserve to live rent-free in her head. Bloody squatter.

After the first chat in the laundrette last week, on the way home, she and Stacey had talked some more. Hailey had offered to buy the knife—it had been surreal that they'd even *had* that type of conversation, that she'd even had the balls to make that decision. She couldn't use any of hers because having one missing out of the pine block would mean Mum would query where it had gone.

Earlier in the week, Hailey had dropped Delaney off at the play centre where Mum worked, seeing as the schools hadn't reopened after Christmas yet, and she'd walked past St Matthew's church towards Asif's Corner Store, the only place she could think of where the owner didn't ask questions, didn't have CCTV, and his eyesight and memory were piss-poor. She doubted he'd even remember her being there as he'd barely paid her any attention, only glancing up briefly to check she was old enough to buy a knife in one of those annoying moulded packages. She'd taken cash from her housekeeping pot, which she had to hide in the shed so Joe didn't get his hands on it.

Joe's face, skewed with anger, barged into her mind again.

"Where's the fucking cash gone?"

"I keep it in the bank now, what with those burglaries last week."

"I need it for the pub, you stupid cow. Go and draw some out."

"I've only got bill money left."

He'd stared at her as if incensed she'd dared to go against him, then stormed out, slamming the door behind him.

Shrugging off the memory, she returned downstairs, flicking the landing and hallway lights off, thinking maybe it would be best to get Delaney out of London tomorrow morning while all this shit was going on. The police were bound to come here—someone would tell them he had a girlfriend, and they'd soon work out who she was. They'd want to ask questions. She shouldn't have Delaney here for that.

Every six weeks he went to stay with Riley's parents in Kent for the weekend. They collected him on Friday nights. Maybe, because they'd gone away for Christmas to Spain and hadn't seen him on Boxing Day when they usually did, they'd be more than happy to take him to theirs tomorrow, even though he wasn't due to go there yet. Would it be rude of her to ask? She couldn't keep relying on Mum.

She fired off a text to them then put the washing she'd done at Lil's in a basket in the kitchen, closing the door so she could do the washing up without waking her son. She'd been that paranoid her mother would try to fix the supposed broken washing machine while she'd been out that she'd pulled it out from beneath the worktop and switched off the plug. Sunday, once all this was over, Hailey would make out she'd got it fixed, because she and Stacey had agreed they wouldn't see each other after that. At least not for a while anyway.

They'd bought cheap throwaway phones with cash from Asif's to keep in touch, but only to send coded messages if it looked like either of them were going to get caught. They'd promised to never send texts from their homes or work, but away from the mast in their area.

The amount of planning they'd had to hash out was unreal.

Her other phone's text tone rang out, and she jumped, even though she'd been expecting a response from Riley's mum and dad. But it could be Joe, sending more threats. She opened the app and sighed in relief. Ken and Polly would collect Delaney in the morning at nine, bringing him back the day before school started. Hailey didn't even have to pack a bag, they had clothes for her son at theirs, and toys, a toothbrush, everything he needed.

Washing up done and a cuppa made, she sat at the two-chair table, praying Joe wouldn't turn up. He'd kick up a fuss because his key wouldn't twist round, plus she'd put the chain on. But she'd made up her mind, he wasn't coming in here again—she had five bolts on the back door now, screwing them on herself last night. When he'd barged in on Wednesday evening, all bluster and a downturned mouth, he'd reminded her not to tell anyone about the rape, pushing her against the wall with his forearm across her throat. He'd examined her cut wrist, licked it, and smiled, as though pleased he'd marked her. Scarred her. She could still feel the scrape of his wet tongue now. Then he'd rambled on about a meet he had tomorrow night at the end of Kitchen Street, nine p.m. Hailey had messaged Stacey about that, and they'd discussed it tonight.

When she'd learned from that bloke that Joe ran a county drug line, in charge of several pushers, her world had kind of skewed. All the lies he'd told her—that he was a carpenter who went away for work on big projects for housing companies, which had explained why he hadn't been coming round so much. In reality, he'd been in London all along, only using her for sex and to bark at, pick fault in.

Well, once he was dead, she was going to give the police an anonymous tip-off using the throwaway phone, telling them exactly who he'd been and that they ought to check the burner that would be found on him. She'd read up about county lines, how each person involved only got hold of one another using cheap pay-as-you-go mobiles, and Joe's phone would be the one customers used to order their fixes. Then Joe's crew, or whatever the fuck he called it, if anything, would be sent out to deliver. Because he ran it, he was making big money, so why the hell did he steal hers? Because he could? For control?

She earned enough to manage. Riley's mum and dad paid her child support in place of their son after his death, proving what lovely people they were. She supposed they only wanted the best for Delaney, didn't want him going without. Riley had been an only child, and Delaney was all they had left of him. Her job, a manager in a clothes shop in town, paid okay, and she got tax credits on top. But in that phase of Joe nicking her housekeeping money from the tin when it had been in her kitchen cupboard, she'd struggled. It had been her food money; she preferred cash for that as she liked going to the market for some things, fruit and veg, fish and meat. But Mum had stepped in to help out. Hailey had lied and said her wages had been dropped rather than tell her Joe had stolen it.

God, the amount of fibs that had passed her lips the past few months because of him. She hated bullshitting Mum, but the shame at falling for a man like Joe meant she couldn't admit anything bad was going on. Plus, it would break Mum's heart, especially because Riley had been the perfect partner. Learning that Joe wasn't, that he was like Dad… No, Hailey couldn't rake up memories of the past for her mother. So really, lying was a kindness.

Anyway, he acts all nice in front of her so she might not believe me.

Hailey couldn't remember her father, he'd buggered off with another woman when she was a baby, but she'd heard the stories, how he used to hit Mum, swaggering around thinking he was the bee's knees. No one Hailey had spoken to had a good word to say about him, although he was apparently charming when you first met him, until the real side came out. Joe must have learned from the same handbook.

She sipped her tea, thinking about tomorrow night. They planned to stab Joe about half past eight, so when whoever he was meeting turned up at nine, he'd be found. Hiding his body wasn't an option, because it had to look like someone had stabbed him then run. The bloke who'd told her what he was up to had said Joe worked at one end of Kitchen these days, away from the sex workers at the other, and as the streetlights had been put out down there—probably by one of Joe's minions so they weren't seen dealing—they'd be safe to approach him in the darkness.

The day after her first visit to the laundrette with Stacey, Hailey had walked down Kitchen with Delaney so she could check the area, see what they'd be dealing with. While there were plenty of houses, the two closest to the end of the row were empty, boarded up. She wondered whether they were 'trap' houses, a name the police used for residences overtaken by dealers, where they stored the drugs. Google had thrown up so much information that she now had a handle on exactly what Joe did and how it worked. And how much cash he likely raked in.

"What I earn is none of your fucking business. If I want to take your money, I will."

So if they were trap houses, did that mean someone would be in there, watching through a knothole in the boards? Would they see Hailey and Stacey, come out and ask them what they were doing? Or would they assume they were buying drugs?

Shit, there was so much to consider. So much that could go wrong. If Joe had stayed the same man he'd been when she'd met him, none of this would be happening. She wasn't a spiteful person, she'd never have dreamed she'd plan to kill someone, but the rape had broken her inside, a stitch missing that she'd never be able to repair.

She struggled to work out when Joe had first turned nasty. She remembered the initial incident, just not exactly when. Maybe her mind had blocked it out. She'd been used to Riley and his kind ways, and Joe had been nice to begin with. She'd put his later moods down to depression—his nan had died not long ago, and he hadn't taken it well.

She'd been so stupid. It all made sense now. He was likely taking a sample of the drugs he supplied which had altered his personality. Still, that wasn't an excuse. He'd chosen to smoke it, or maybe sniff it up his nose, perhaps to numb the pain of his nan's passing, so it wasn't Hailey's fault, like he made out.

She finished her tea, inspecting her wrist. It still had scabs a week on. She should have had butterfly stitches really, but going to hospital to get those done would have brought questions she didn't want to answer, as would buying them from the chemist. Pharmacists were a nosy bunch lately. Because of the way he'd carved the rhombus, or diamond as Stacey had called it, one pointed end went over onto the base of her hand near her thumb, so it meant she'd spent the week wearing her cardigan with extra-long sleeves so it hid the mess. Eagle-eyed Delaney had spotted it, pushing her sleeve up, but she'd told him she'd scraped it on a brick wall, and he'd wandered off after that, focusing on his toys instead.

She'd get a tattoo when the cuts had healed, like Stacey had. Flowers, maybe a little butterfly hovering above them, to show she'd flown from the chrysalis Joe had swaddled around her.

Did the rhombus mean anything? Or *was* it a diamond? It reminded her of the block-type writing graffiti artists used, an 'O' on the wonk. Maybe it didn't mean anything at all, he'd just created a frame to put the J inside. She was probably reading too much into it, so she shoved it out of her mind, covering her wrist so she didn't have to see it.

At half eleven, after more tea and more thoughts, the faint sound of a key sliding into the lock in the front door had her shoving her almost-empty cup away in fright. It landed on its side at the edge of the table, saved from falling by the handle acting as a stopper. Liquid spilled onto the wood. Her mouth went dry, her heartbeat going crazy, and she stood, hands shaking, noodle legs. She rushed to the back door to check Mum hadn't gone out the back for a ciggie when she'd been here, forgetting to lock it after. No, all was secure, and the blinds were down on the door and window, so even if Joe went into her garden, he wouldn't be able to see her.

But the light was on, so he might see her shape.

She flicked it off, opened the internal door, and poked her head round the jamb. Only a night light glowed by the front door at the bottom of the stairs, but her outside lamp was on, pasting Joe's silhouette. The one in the living room was out, the door closed, so maybe he'd think she'd gone to bed.

The letterbox flap opened, and his shadow moved lower.

"Let me in, you stupid fucking slag."

He didn't shout, so had he already prowled in the back garden and seen the light on? Or did he know she'd likely be awake anyway, reading her Kindle, and she'd have heard him? The menace in his tone sent a shiver through her. She clamped her lips shut, trembling not only with fear that he'd smash the glass in the door panel and undo the chain and double lock, but also with anger, the fact he thought it was okay to call her that. Taking drugs or not, he didn't have the right to treat her like shit.

This had been going on for too long now, and like she'd said tonight to Stacey, she wasn't going to put up with it. Living in near-constant panic had done a number on her nerves, and if she allowed it to continue any longer, she'd be put on tablets.

Maybe she should forget killing him and ring the police later, tell them everything. But her worry over his gang of runners coming after her for getting him arrested, if he even was…who knew how many there were, and the outfit who sold Joe the drugs might also catch up with her. She had to protect Delaney from seeing that kind of violence should they break in and attack her.

They might wait for a while before they acted out their revenge, too, giving her a false sense of security.

Death was the only answer.

"If you'd fucked off on holiday, you wouldn't have put the chain on the door," he said, "so I know you're in there."

Was he thick? She could have left via the back to avoid being seen if he'd sent someone here to watch her house.

"Haaaaaiiiley!" he called. "Open. The. Fucking. Door."

She breathed deeply, calming her racing heart, praying Delaney didn't wake up and give the game away.

"What are ye feckin' doin'?" someone else said. "Feck off out of here."

Joe's silhouette rose, although he kept the letterbox open, the ends of his fingers poking inside. If she wasn't scared of the repercussions, she'd grab her cleaver from the knife block and chop the fuckers off.

"Who the fuck are you?" Joe said, fingers twitching where he likely wanted to do the bloke some damage.

"No one. Just move on."

"Are you her new bit on the side?"

"Whose?"

"Her in there."

"I don't know who lives there. All I heard was ye tellin' whoever it is tae open the feckin' door, aggressive like, and ye really ought not tae be doin' that."

"Who says?"

"I expect The Brothers would have somethin' tae say about it. Didn't ye know she's under their protection?"

What? Hailey swallowed.

"How come?" Joe asked.

"I don't know, but everyone down this street is, as of today. Maybe the twins have a vested interest—maybe girls will be set up on the corner. Either way, ye need tae take ye fingers out of that letterbox and piss off."

Joe didn't remove them right away, waiting a few seconds, which was all that was needed to prove his point—that he'd do it when *he* wanted to. "What are you, some kind of enforcer?" he asked, voice somewhat dulled.

"Somethin' like that."

"Huh. Fucking Irish tosser. Go back to where you came from."

Joe's shape disappeared, but the man's remained. He leaned his back on the side of her door, as if standing guard. Hailey approached, lifting the letterbox flap.

"Are you staying there all night?" she asked.

"Ah, so ye're awake. No, I'm waitin' for someone tae come and keep watch on the street. That's what happens when the twins own it."

"Is it true, what you said about them?"

"That ye're under their protection? Yeah."

"How come?"

"I have no idea. I just do as I'm told. Go tae bed. Ye'll be all right now."

She climbed the stairs and went into her room, looking out through a crack in the curtains. The man had left her door and now stood at the kerb, an orange glow draped over him from the light of the lamppost. Beard. Baggy, scruffy clothes. Fucking hell, it was the one from the laundrette! What was *he* doing here?

He stayed there for a while, as did she, waiting for whoever would turn up.

A car arrived and parked opposite, another bearded man in the driver's seat. They waved at each other, then Mr Irish Scruffy walked off in the direction of town. The other remained, staring ahead in the direction Joe had gone.

All the houses on this side belonged to Mr Partridge who'd bought them when Hailey had been a little girl. Had he sold them to the twins? Would they all get a letter about the change of landlord? Would her rent go up? Would she have to also pay protection money?

Whatever it was, it bothered her. Having someone sitting out there in a car at random times would mean she'd be seen coming and going tomorrow night.

Fuck.

Chapter Five

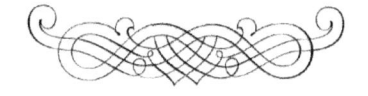

Amy Osbourne knew her thirteen-year-old son wasn't right in the head, but there was nothing she could do about it. Her husband, Pete, would batter her if she approached the school or the doctor for help, and Joe would likely slap her an' all. For years, those two had bullied her, Pete more than Joe, admittedly. She 'knew her place'. Didn't mean she liked living

there, though, and she was going to do something about it. She'd woken up years ago, knew exactly what was right and what was wrong in her life, but she hid that in front of Pete and Joe. Played docile because she had revenge in her heart, and she'd stay with them until she'd enacted it. She'd be beaten up again and again in order to have the last laugh. Stubborn of her, stupid, but the seed had been planted, and she couldn't stop the damn thing from growing.

The day she'd admitted defeat, that she was a battered, controlled woman, she'd packed a bag and hidden round her friend's house for a week, without Joe, working out where she'd live and work, planning a new life. Out of London, definitely. But her old man had found her. Dragged her back home. It was then her evil streak had woken up and she'd told herself to stay and get back at Pete. Some would say she wasn't right in the head, let alone her son, to put herself through this, but by now that seed had turned into an unruly weed, then into big, strangling vines with thick stalks and grasping, tendril-like offshoots that gripped every facet of her.

She'd kill him or go down trying, no matter how long it took.

She'd been working at Lil's Laundrette for years, her only solace in her otherwise horrible days. Too afraid to tell anyone at first about her home life, she'd played that game where everything looked fine to outsiders—still did. It was exhausting, making out to Mum and Dad that Pete was the love of her life and provided everything she'd ever wanted. Pete behaved himself in front of them, as did Joe, but as soon as they left their company, the nightmare resumed.

Her friend and neighbour, Belinda, knew what was going on, and recently, Amy had opened up to Lil, but in a sneaky way, using the age-old 'I've got this friend, and I need advice for her' excuse as a way to get someone else's perspective on the life she lived. To know whether her thoughts and feelings were valid. Like the fact she wished Pete was dead and Joe wasn't her son.

She stared at Joe's bedroom walls. Pete said the lad was 'expressing himself' and 'leave him the fuck alone', but Amy reckoned it was outright disrespect, what that boy had done. He'd ruined the white paintwork with graffiti, each strange block a different colour, all outlined in black. Pete had provided the money for the spray paint, such a waste of cash, yet said he never had any spare money when she asked for it.

There was always spare for the pub, though.

The wall pattern was a honeycomb of what might be diamonds locked together, the letter J in the middles of most but interspersed with the word 'rhombus'. Shapes were relevant in their household, they all had one, some weird thing of Pete's. But why was Joe a rhombus? This mess was to do with a gang, apparently, some kind of tag, whatever that was, and Amy should have known Joe would end up in one of those awful thuggish groups. He was the leader, and that made perfect sense, too. Pete had taught him well, too well, and while at home Joe was the disciple, outside of it he was Jesus, the one everyone followed.

He'd been such a placid baby, a lovely kid up until around three years old when Pete's lessons had started. "Go and slap Mummy" and "Pinch her face" had been the beginning of it, then Pete teaching him defiance, but only against her. When Pete was out of the house, Amy had tried to bring Joe up the right way, but it was as if a mental block had prevented her son from soaking up any kind of goodness. It creeped her out how that child could act so differently at primary school, the teacher praising Amy for rearing such a 'dear' boy, and in secondary, his sometimes recalcitrant behaviour (when his mask slipped?) had been put down to him being a teenager, hormones, all that rubbish.

She had no control over him whatsoever.

No control over anything apart from at work and her plans to kill his father.

Maybe Rhombus was the gang's name. Or, she thought with dread, Joe was following in Pete's footsteps by adopting that stupid shape analogy. Pete was a star, the self-appointed name he'd given himself, the reason obvious, and Amy was a kite. He'd laughingly told her that was because he held the string, directing her movements, and while it appeared to anyone watching she was able to fly high, she was still tethered. He must have told Joe about it, and he'd chosen rhombus. But what did that mean?

She shouldn't care, not with how Joe verbally beat her down as much as his father did. If she were a decent mother, she'd want to save her son before it was too late. Could she undo all of Pete's evil work, though? Surely it was too ingrained in Joe for her to reach him now.

She looked around, anger prodding at her. Joe was spoiled, not just as a person but with material things. Pete had always bribed him to misbehave with lures, gifts, the latest being a laptop all to himself. He no longer had to use the old-fashioned yellowing computer downstairs, the monitor with its blocky back, which Pete used to play Solitaire and scour filthy websites. He didn't hide it from her, preferring to taunt her by showing the images of perfect women in sexual poses, informing her, "Look how much you've let yourself go." It was disgusting, him ogling women, and he did it in front of Joe, too, gesturing for him to come over and "Have a look at the tits on that, son."

Amy sighed and made Joe's bed. He'd gone to school, and Pete was at work, and in the limited time she had before she needed to be at the laundrette, she dashed around the house, tidying and making sure everything was just so, then hung a load of washing on the line. Pete and Joe didn't like mess, the pair of them so weirdly anal about it yet never lifting a finger to keep the place nice themselves.

"Of course they fucking don't, they've got me as their skivvy," she muttered and slid her arms into her lightweight jacket.

Spring had arrived, the sun was out in a clear blue sky, daffodils sprouting their yellow-bell heads, a signal for new beginnings. If she had her way, she'd have a new beginning and Pete would meet his end, but she still hadn't figured out how to do that. Whichever way she tried to kill him, she'd likely get caught.

She left the house and walked down Blanchard Crescent towards the exit. Belinda, who lived a couple of doors down in number one, opened her front door and scuttled to the end of her garden path. Amy stopped to talk. Five minutes wouldn't hurt, and she could always up her pace to work after. Mind you, Lil wouldn't say anything if she was late, she was good like that.

"Her next door said Pete was at it again last night." Belinda jerked her head to the house between hers and Amy's. "Said she heard the majority of it through the wall—more likely standing there with a glass against it, you know what she's like. She's going to ring the police next time."

"Let her. Maybe a night in the nick for beating me up will teach him a lesson." *That was a lie, he'd come out fighting twice as hard, but at least Amy would get some respite.*

"This can't keep happening, you know that, don't you? He's going to go too far one day." Belinda came closer so they could speak quietly. "There has to be some way you can get rid of him."

Oh, there was, but Amy couldn't tell Belinda. Couldn't tell anybody. How did one confess to planning a murder? Did you just blurt it? "Maybe he'll drop dead one day, his blood pressure must be raging, and seeing as arsenic doesn't come in convenient little bottles these days, there's not much I can do but wait."

"I'd fucking suffocate him in his sleep. If my Roger treated me like that, I'd sit on the pillow until he stopped breathing."

Roger. He had a lot to answer for. Amy would quite like to kill him, too.

She laughed. *"Hmm, but then the police would know what I'd done. Post-mortems, don't forget. I'd be carted away, then what would happen to Joe? I wouldn't want to foist him on my mum and dad, or Pete's. Then again, they think he's an angel, and he'd behave for them. He acts like butter wouldn't melt when we see them."*

Belinda shook her head in consternation. *"That boy is something else. Sneaky. He stuck his middle finger up to me the other day. I don't know how you've got the patience to put up with either of them. Still, at least Pete hasn't made you one of those poor cows who goes around like a zombie, completely controlled by him. You know it's wrong, what he does, so that's half the battle. There's that women's refuge you could try, but I suppose they'd expect you to take Joe with you."*

Belinda knew damn well how Amy felt about her son. She never judged, she understood how you could love someone yet dislike them, and besides, Joe wouldn't want to be with Amy, he'd choose Pete every time.

"Not necessarily. They must take in women with no kids. Anyway, what's the point in talking about it? Pete would only find me."

"Nah, they'd do one of those things like witness protection, wouldn't they? Hide you, give you a new name. I can't for the life of me think what the local charity's called, but they get you a new house and all sorts."

It was tempting, to walk away from it all and start again, but why should Amy be the one to run? She wasn't a bitch to either of them, and it was her house as much as it was Pete's, she'd always contributed to the mortgage, so why would she leave it all behind? No, she'd rather he died.

"I'll think about it," she said. "I'd best get on."

"You know where I am if you need me." Belinda walked up her path.

Amy continued out of the crescent and headed to work. She imagined ways of killing Pete without any blame landing at her door. A car crash, but she had no idea how to engineer that. Him tripping and landing on a knife, the blade preferably sticking into his neck. An intruder, bashing the shit out of his head with a hammer, except it would be her in her nightie and slippers.

She smiled at the thought and entered the laundrette, the scent of various washing powders hitting her. She loved that clean smell and the sounds of the machines humming. Both signified she was in her haven. A few women were in, no kids as they were at school, some reading magazines, others with chunky books in hand.

Lil stood behind the counter, glancing up and smiling at Amy. "Morning, mucker. I'll make us a cuppa, then I'll be off after that. Got to see a man about a dog."

She followed Amy into the staffroom and got on with the brew. Amy hung her handbag and jacket up. Once Lil had gone, she'd take over the service washes. There would be clothes to fold and pack into laundry bags, ready for customers to collect. She liked that job, it was mundane and gave her time to dream about a life without Pete and Joe in it, but she also enjoyed nosing at other people's outfits. Sometimes that dragged her mood down, though, it brought home how dowdy she'd become, how her clothes had no colour. Seeing Lil was the same. That woman loved the outrageous and today had a black leather skirt and a zebra-print blouse on, her long wavy hair dyed orange.

"How's your abused friend?" Lil asked over the kettle clanking then rumbling.

"She got beat up again last night."

"Poor cow. I'm surprised she didn't turn around and slit her husband's throat."

"She said she thought about it. Reckoned she'd only get a short stint in the nick because it would have been self-defence, plus she's a battered woman so the judge would feel sorry for her."

"Makes you wonder why she didn't, then."

Amy looked over at Lil who eyed her funny. Shit, did she know all these stories were about herself? Amy had been so careful to keep any emotion out of her voice when she spoke about the abuse.

"She's got a child, I told you." Amy sat at the little table. "Despite disliking the kid, she can't leave her with him." She'd felt it best to say a daughter was involved, not a son, thinking that would throw Lil right off the scent, but the subterfuge had likely been a waste of time as Lil seemed to know what Amy had been playing at.

"What did he do to her this time? And what did she do to 'deserve' it?" Lil poured boiled water then squeezed a teabag against the side of a cup.

"She burnt the beans. He punched her in the stomach. She fell to the floor, so he kicked her in the thigh. It fucking hurt."

"Tell you that, did she?"

Amy flushed at her fuck-up. "Well, I wouldn't know otherwise."

Lil poured milk. "It's just that you said 'it fucking hurt' like you knew exactly how much. Like it happened to you."

"Me?" Amy slapped a hand to her chest and trotted out a silly laugh.

Lil brought the teas over and sat. "Listen, I've played along so you had someone to talk to, but this is getting too often now, Pete hitting you."

"But Pete doesn't hit me."

"He does. I saw you wincing last week while you were folding washing—when you said your friend was punched in the ribs. I'm not going to tell anyone if that's what you're worried about. I've got secrets inside me you wouldn't believe, but I'll tell you this much for nothing, it isn't as hard to kill someone and get rid of the body as you might think."

Amy's stomach went south. "What?"

"You heard me. And you've said yourself, your friend has been entertaining how she can kill her old man." Lil sipped her drink. Cradled the cup. "You know I was one of Ron Cardigan's Treacles back in the day. I learned a hell of a lot from him, and getting rid of Pete will be a piece of piss. There's this place I know. You could dump his body there."

There was no point in continuing this pretence. "But he's massive. I wouldn't be able to carry him. And one of the neighbours would see me putting him in the car, even if I did it in the middle of the night. They're all so nosy and get out of bed at the slightest sound."

"Not if you didn't kill him at home — and don't tell me you haven't entertained it because I won't fucking believe you."

"Where would I do it, though?"

"He drinks in the Red Lion, right?"

"Right…"

"Someone might just happen to waylay him when he leaves there, know what I mean?"

"Who? Me?"

"No, you need to be at home with your kid for an alibi, and if Joe goes out, then you get yourself round Belinda's for a cuppa. I could rustle up a couple of men for you, but you'd have to pay them."

"I don't have that kind of money."

"No, but when the life insurance pays out…" Lil paused. "You do have policies, don't you?"

"Yes, but… Oh God. I can't believe we're talking about this."

"You can trust me. I'm a safe bet, believe me. You've been working here for bloody years, and I've never told anyone anything you've said, have I?"

"No."

"Well then. Talk to me. Tell me how you'd *do it."*

"What about the service washes?"

"The machines won't be finished for another hour."

"What about that man about a dog?"

"It can wait."

Amy took a deep breath. "I've been…I've been upping his salt intake for months, but it hasn't done anything. He's meant to have become confused and jittery according to Google, but he hasn't. Later on, he could go into a coma."

"Have you noticed him drinking a lot more?"

"Well, yes, but…"

"Then he thinks he's just thirsty and it's flushing the salt out of his system before it has a chance to cause much damage. How much salt are you giving him?"

"I started with adding a quarter of a teaspoon to his dinner at first, so he didn't notice, then upped it as time went on once he was used to the taste. I'm at two teaspoons in bolognaise and chilli now—I stir it into his after I've dished mine and Joe's up."

"It's not enough, and if he dies they'll do blood tests, and the sodium will show up. Then, as the one who

makes the dinner, you'll be the first they suspect. Pack it in. Doesn't he comment that his grub's salty?"

"Yes, but with me and Joe saying ours is fine, he thinks his taste buds are up the swanny."

"No more salt, okay? We'll do something else."

"What, though?"

"Like I said, a couple of men..."

Amy shook her head. "I'm scared of someone else knowing it's me who ordered it to happen. It's bad enough that you *know because it means you're complicit. I'm a horrible person for wanting him dead rather than just walking out. And before you suggest I do that, it didn't work last time."*

"What happened?"

"I camped out at Belinda's, but he found out where I was and took me home."

"I expect her husband told him. Roger's a bit of a twat like that."

"Yes, it was him."

"Was that the time you took a week off, saying you were ill?"

"Yes. Sorry I lied."

"Not a problem, but had I known why you were really off, I'd have had you round my gaff. We could have found you a flat out of London, got you well away. Which brings me to Joe. I know you said your

friend hates her daughter, but we don't need to hide behind that anymore. You hate Joe, yes?"

"I can't bear him. He's a mini version of Pete. I feel so bad about it, I'm his mother, I'm meant to love him unconditionally, but I'm scared of him. His eyes go black when he's angry, and that's not normal."

"My mum used to say that was the Devil living inside people."

Amy shivered. "There's something inside him all right."

"Evil."

"Hmm."

They drank their tea for a bit, Amy relieved she didn't have to lie to Lil anymore. It felt so good to have spoken about this, admitting it was happening to her, not some fictitious mate, but it worried her that she'd be implicated in what Lil had suggested—or worse, Lil got arrested, too.

Amy finished her tea. "It could work, those men going after Pete, but I'd be stuck with Joe, and I can't handle him. He hits me, too."

"What? Fucking hell's bells, that's not right. I wouldn't stoop low enough to suggest they bump Joe of an' all, but they could scare him into behaving."

"I think it's too late for that. He's awful. I can't explain it, but he's not right in the head. He's got a fair few cogs missing."

"Leave it with me. If you're sure you want Pete gone, I'll arrange it. I'll say it's me who wants him dead, not you."

Amy bit her lip. "The life insurance money might take a while to come through, though."

"That's all right. They'll wait. They happen to be good friends of mine and might well do it for free if they think it's me who wants it done. I'll let you know." Lil rose and put her coat on, the beige suede one with the white furry collar. "Now, I'm off to see when it can be done, that dog can wait."

Amy wondered what the 'dog' was, what Lil was up to other than arranging a murder.

Lil smiled. "You act normal, okay?"

"Okay." Amy stood. "Thank you."

"You're welcome. Now get out there and fold Mr Sugden's massive skiddy underpants or I'll sack you."

Lil left the room, laughing, and it set Amy off, too.

Come next week, Pete might be dead.

She could hardly believe her luck.

Chapter Six

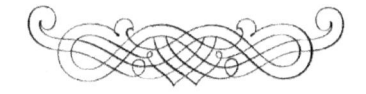

Incensed because of Hailey being such a stupid bitch, Joe made his way back to Kitchen Street on foot. He didn't fancy going home to his poky flat. He wouldn't be able to sleep, what with all this anger surging through him, and sitting up playing mindless shit on his Xbox would piss him off because the online gamers got on his tits. Kids who ran their mouths off. Mind you, he could take his irritation out on them, give them a bit of verbal, but he risked them reporting him and having his membership revoked. His boss said he was nothing but a big kid, still gaming at his age, but fucking hell, he was only twenty-two.

He stomped on, his mind whirring. Who the fuck did Hailey think she was, hiding in her house like that? Who'd given her permission to do that? What right did she have? She must have put the double-lock snib down on the Yale because his key hadn't turned. He'd warned her not to do that, telling her he could come and go as he damn well pleased, yet she'd defied him. He reckoned it was the rape that had done it. Women tended to get a bit shirty when he did that. It had sent her nutty, and she was behaving irrationally as a result.

What was it with birds who thought they could have a mind of their own? His mum had tried it with his dad, the stupid cow growing a backbone. Dad had soon knocked it out of her, and the black eye as a result had meant she hadn't left the house all weekend.

Women should know their place, and that was to do as they were fucking well told. Mum had, there hadn't been a peep out of her since, all "Yes, Pete. No, Pete," like it should always be. Joe wanted a missus like that.

He walked round the back of the trap house at the end of the road, peering into the darkness of the garden to make sure no one lurked. Some skag-headed wanker must have followed Joe here once, and a week later, he'd turned up trying to get some gear on tick. Joe had had to beat seven bells out of him to show him he wasn't welcome around here, nor could he tell anyone where the base was.

Joe twitched. He needed a fix badly. He'd have a sniff then bag up some drugs, that'd keep his mind occupied, and it'd save him having to do it tomorrow, ready for the Saturday night rush. If he didn't do something productive, he was likely to go back to Hailey's and kill her, *and* that whiny kid of hers. Spoiled little shit. Fucking slag. And that Irish bloke. Did he really work for the twins, or was that an elaborate cover story for the fact he'd been shagging her?

Being confronted like that had wound Joe right up. He didn't like being told what to do, but he'd sensed if he didn't walk away, Paddy would have beaten the crap out of him. He had that air about him of someone who wouldn't blink over snapping your neck. As Joe valued his—he didn't want to end up in a wheelchair, numb from the waist down—he'd done as asked. It had naffed him off, though. The only person he allowed to tell him what to do was Dad and his boss, Galaxy.

Thank God Hailey didn't have any brothers, nor did she have many friends with fellas who could do him over, warn him away. He'd made sure she'd sacked her mates off. You couldn't control your woman if she had other women twittering in her ear. Stacey's brothers had roughed him up something chronic, breaking a rib with their kicks, giving him a concussion from their boots to his head, his face a mass of bruising and split lips. He'd done the sensible thing and never went back to her house after that, steered well clear of her, but the need to kill her had boiled inside him until he'd met Hailey. Concentrating all his efforts on her had erased his need to teach Stacey a lesson, but given the chance, he still would.

She had a new partner now, a rich one, older than her, and she'd moved into his gaff. Joe could get a big house like that, but splashing out would draw attention to himself. Better that he stayed in his manky, mould-infested flat. People needed to think he was on benefits, some scruff who couldn't be arsed to work full-time for a living, and the ruse he was a carpenter as a cash-in-hand side hustle meant Hailey hadn't asked questions about him going away on jobs—until she'd started questioning him recently. She'd found out about the drugs, and it had royally narked him. Someone had also implied he shagged women on Kitchen Street, but so what if he did? None of Hailey's business.

Running a county line was king-like on one hand and fraught with nerves on the other. While he was the boss of the runners, *he* also had a boss, so he had to watch how he behaved else he'd get shanked by him. Galaxy had a selection of knives, including a machete, and he never hesitated to use them.

Joe's life was full of people who annoyed him. As well as Hailey becoming a fly in the ointment, someone he couldn't control as much as he'd thought, there was that bastard copper, Flint, who bribed him for money. Joe had been his unofficial informant for a while, giving him tip-offs about other drug runners not on the line's payroll, all so he could send his own in to take their places and custom.

"If you don't give me five hundred quid, I'll nick you, get you sent down for a fucking long stretch because we both know exactly what you're up to."

"I haven't got five hundred on me!"

"A hundred a week will do, but remember, if you don't give it to me, you're fucked, got it?"

"Okay, okay!"

"Hand the first instalment over, then."

Wanker. Flint needed a mega kicking, but he had Joe by the balls, and besides, Galaxy wanted the copper on their side. Joe would bet Flint had been watching, taking photos and videos, then he could make out he'd been undercover in his spare time and tell his colleagues Joe ran the line. Then again, he wouldn't be able to syphon money out of Joe anymore, and the pig loved the readies.

Now Joe thought about it, the cash Flint gave him for info was then given back for the bribes, so being a grass was pointless. Maybe now was the time to say to Galaxy that informing Flint about other runners wasn't working anymore. He'd have to put it in a way that he wasn't telling the boss what to do, though. Galaxy had a wicked temper.

Gloves on, Joe entered the trap house using a key in the lock he'd had fitted, smiling at the power he had over his runners, like Galaxy had power over him. Every single one of them had been lured in to work for him with the promise of riches, of belonging to his 'family'. On their first nights, Galaxy had arranged for them to be robbed, the stolen drugs and money going back into the line. Then the runners were told it was their responsibility to make sure no one stole the gear, so it was their duty to pay it back. Free labour, because nobody got paid until the nicked cash had been recouped.

By then, they were so desperate to earn, having seen how much the sales raked in, they continued peddling, hooked on the money as much as the customers were hooked on drugs.

Joe locked himself in and went to the kitchen area where he had a camping stove. He filled the kettle, lit the gas, and popped it on top. A coffee would help keep him awake.

He inspected his new tattoo on the back of his hand, done today. He'd removed the annoying clingfilm shite on the top and washed it, but it was sore as eff, the skin being so thin. It was a 3D quadrilateral, the shape matching who he was perfectly—formed by four sides, something that had caught his eye while browsing on his phone once upon a time, plus Dad had told him to pick a shape that represented him. *Joe* had four sides to him: the son; the bully lover; the line manager; and the person who waited inside him to come out, the one who'd be rich as fuck and moved to Spain to live a life of luxury. How he'd take his savings with him, he wasn't sure yet. He'd stashed it in Hailey's loft in a massive suitcase—putting that amount every week in the bank wasn't an option. So far, he had a good few thousand over a million, but he wanted at least four more.

He'd speak to Galaxy about how to get it into one of those dodgy bank accounts, but he didn't want the bloke to know he planned on scarpering. Maybe he could say he didn't like having all that cash hanging around instead. Yeah, that'd work.

The kettle whistled, and he made his drink. Sat at the bench running the length of the back wall in the dining area where he prepped all the baggies. He already had a block of coke there waiting, the rest for tomorrow night upstairs in a safe. He only kept four blocks here at a time, the same with weed. The rest was stored in Galaxy's lock-up, which he accessed via a code on a keypad. There was no chance of nicking a cheeky brick for himself because the bloody place had cameras installed inside. Galaxy trusted no one.

A tap on the back door had the hairs at the nape of his neck going up. Annoyed he hadn't had a chance to snort some cocaine, he checked the camera app on his phone to see who was there, anger bursting at the sight of that stupid, *stupid* prick with his head down so he wasn't captured on film.

Christ, this was all he needed.

He let Flint in, locking the door again. "What the fuck do you want *now*?"

Flint stared at him as though he thought of him as a daft kid, a youngster who got on his nerves. Joe supposed he *was* a kid to him, seeing as Flint must be in his forties.

"Well, if you don't want me to pass on a bit of gossip that would be to your advantage, I'll just go, shall I?"

Joe studied the copper. He wasn't messing. Whatever had gone on was serious. Joe hated the fact he needed whatever information Flint could give, but he tried not to show that in his expression.

"What's happened?" He picked up his cup to give his hand something to do other than punching Flint in his smug face. He imagined the crunch of bone and cartilage and almost smiled, but that would give Flint the wrong impression, so he schooled his features into a mask of nothing.

Flint smirked. "I heard The Brothers are onto the line."

"What do you mean, onto? Like, Galaxy has brought them in on it?" That was fucking annoying. The boss should have let him know about this.

"No, as in they know it exists and are gunning for whoever runs it."

Joe's stomach rolled over. "How do they know?"

"Search me."

"How did you find out?"

"Whispers, you know how it is."

"Shit." Joe didn't need this crap. "What about the police investigation? How's that going?"

"There's a sting operation going off Monday, early hours. They're just getting their ducks in a row first. The runners are being rounded up—yours and all the others. It won't take long for them to blab about the trap house."

Joe and Galaxy had scared the life out of the pushers, but what if the police scared them more? He sighed. This base had been perfect because Flint had put feelers out with the council to see how long Joe could use it for. The two boarded-up houses weren't being revamped until new funds came in six months down the line, and now he'd have to find another one. He always had gloves on in here, but his DNA could be found by way of a hair, a speck of flaked skin, some shit like that. He'd arrange for it to be scrubbed. Get everything out by Sunday. Saturday was their busiest night, and he didn't have time to relocate by tomorrow.

"Cheers for the heads-up. How come they know about the runners? The cops, I mean."

Flint tutted. "Are you dim? They've got people out there watching the streets at night."

Joe used couriers to deliver the gear to the runners in alleyways or places out of sight, the same with collecting the takings which were then put in Galaxy's lock-up. The thought of the rozzers prowling, knowing who worked for Joe, did his nut in. He'd followed Galaxy's rules to the letter, a tried-and-tested method, a solid operation, but privately, Joe had thought kids speeding around on bikes with their hoods up and Covid masks on was fucking dumb, and obvious what they were doing. Seemed he'd been right. The police knew what to look for, and they'd bloody well found it.

He rubbed his tingling nose — he badly needed a bit of sniff. "I suppose you want money for that information."

"Of course I do."

Is this info even legit? Or has he made it up just so I pay him?

"How much?"

"A grand. And before you complain, I'm saving your arse here."

"No, you're saving your cash cow, that's what you're doing. You'll have to wait until I pay you the ton from the other bribe. Like I told you before, I don't carry much cash on me, only runners do that."

Flint shoved him in the chest. Joe's hip slammed against the workbench, pain spiking. Christ, he wanted to kill this motherfucker.

"Listen to me, you wanking scrote." Flint's breath smelled of beer. "I've got untold pressures since I last saw you. Believe me, my back's against the fucking wall in ways you'd never comprehend. My life changed in the blink of a bastard eye, and I have to do as I'm told whether I like it or not."

"What do you mean?"

"Never you mind, but I've got eyes on me, and if I fuck up, I'm dead. Literally."

Had Galaxy got hold of him and had a word? Joe had told the boss that Flint was getting a bit too big for his boots, but Galaxy had said that was tough, having a nasty copper on your side was better than none at all. Flint was their snoop, the man who told them when the shit might hit the fan, and Galaxy had snarled that Joe just had to put up with it. But it sounded like he'd had a change of heart if Flint was worried about being killed.

Joe laughed. "Like that, is it?" Chuffed Galaxy had his back after all, he tutted in derision. "Then you'd best behave yourself, hadn't you."

Flint shook his head, jaw clenching. "I tell you, if I could get away with clubbing your scrawny, nasty little arse without Galaxy getting on my back, I would. I'd even go so far as to bump you off."

"But you can't, can you. We're stuck with each other, so deal with it."

Flint seemed like he had something even more cutting to say but had thought better of it. "I want the money tomorrow morning, and don't tell me you need to pay in instalments because you're bound to have a stash somewhere, so I'll take the rest of what you owe me an' all. It's probably at that girlfriend's of yours. If you don't give me what I want, I'll whisper in The Brothers' ears."

Joe didn't doubt it. Flint was such a mean cunt. He took cuts off all the runners, scaring them shitless with threats to dob them in to the police or the twins. He had a nice earner going, and even if he killed Joe he wouldn't lose out because he'd latch on to the next line manager.

"Ten o'clock in The Angel," Joe said.

"Why in a public place?"

"Because I don't trust you anymore. You've just admitted you want to kill me. I'd be thick as pig shit if I met you somewhere else. If you want that money, you'll do it."

"Fine, but don't make it obvious you're passing me cash."

Joe shrugged. "Whatever, now piss off, I've got work to do." He unlocked the door and gestured for Flint to leave.

The copper glared at him. "I'll have you one day, you smarmy prick. Watch your back."

A frisson of fear wended down Joe's spine, but he bluffed his way through his reply, putting on bravado. "Yeah, watch yours an' all. You never know who you might meet in the dark, piggy."

He locked himself in, Flint's earlier words coasting through his mind.

"I heard The Brothers are onto the line."

Jesus fucking wept.

Chapter Seven

George sighed at the work burner ringing. He'd just got into bed, knackered, and cursed the fact he and Greg ran an Estate which meant they were on call all the time. Still, if Ichabod was phoning, it had to be serious otherwise he'd just send a message.

George swiped to answer. "All right, mate?"

"No. I've been wrestlin' wid whether tae tell ye somethin'."

"Why wrestling?"

"Because I was told in confidence and it happened in Ron's day, so technically, ye don't need tae know, do ye?"

George clamped his jaw shut. Any mention of Ron sent his blood pressure soaring. That bloke had been an arsehole through and through. Him being his father was a serious bugbear, one that would never go away. A tongue probing a sore tooth. You didn't like the pain but poked about anyway. "Depends whether it has any impact on us."

"That's what I said, and she assured me it didn't. I have tae say, since hearin' her story, I'm inclined tae agree wid her, but...I don't like keepin' secrets from ye, and she's a resident, so..."

"...you feel we ought to know anyway."

"Yeah. I'll never admit tae her I've told ye, else she'll never trust me again."

George's suspicions fired up. Of all the things Ichabod could have done, he prayed it wasn't this. "Don't tell me you went back to Hailey's and spoke to her."

"No, I waited for Will tae come, like ye said, then went home."

Will hadn't reported that the man at Hailey's door had come back, so all was well there, but it didn't take a rocket scientist to twig the gobby bloke was the one she planned to murder. With no CCTV at the Noodle and beyond for a few streets, Bennett, who George had contacted to check the cameras, hadn't been able to ascertain who he was, nor where the second blonde had gone. Not surprising regarding her, the same had happened last week. While they now knew who Hailey was via Lil—and he'd be having a word with her for following Ichabod—they were still clueless as to who her accomplice was. So if it wasn't Hailey who'd confessed something...

The light bulb clicked on for him. "Lil."

"Yeah. After Noelle left Hailey's, she went all funny, like she'd seen a ghost. She said she needed a drink, so we went tae the Red Lion."

"And?"

The story pouring out of Ichabod's mouth astounded George. He'd always known Lil was a live wire, she had a mouth on her, but this? Murder?

"You did the right thing by telling me. This Hailey business, and Noelle being involved in Lil's past… I doubt very much it'll impact what we've got planned for tomorrow night, but knowledge is power. So how were things left between Lil and Noelle?"

"As ye can imagine, Noelle was steamin' about Lil havin' an affair wid her old man, but as far as anyone's concerned, he walked out on Noelle for pastures new wid *another* woman."

"Right. Well, let's hope this doesn't return to bite us in the arse at some point. All the more reason for Lil not to go down Princeton Avenue—you said she knew Noelle lived there, so you'd think she'd have fucked off back to the laundrette at that point, not hung around."

"Tae be fair, she wasn't tae know Noelle is Hailey's mammy."

"No, but she's pissed me off by going after you. All for what, a bit of excitement, you said? Stupid bint."

"Right, if she tells me anythin' else, I'll pass it on."

"Good. Now get some sleep. Tomorrow night's a big one."

George ended the call and stomped down the landing to Greg's room. He blundered in, plonking his arse on the bed.

"Oh God. What?" Greg said, sleepy.

"Guess who's got a dark secret?"

"Is this one of those times where you could have waited until the morning?" Greg rolled onto his side, away from George. "Jesus, bruv, it's late."

"Yeah, but I need to tell you about it."

"Why now?"

"Because I'm fucking bursting!"

Greg turned back and sat up. "I swear to God, this had better be worth it."

George told him about the two murders Lil had committed. "What do you think of *that*, then?"

"Blimey, I'd never have had her down as a killer."

"No. She mentioned Noelle's husband but not who the other bloke was. I wonder who it is? What is she, a black widow? And there was you saying I could get together with her just so I had a bird on my arm. Sod that. I'd end up dead."

Greg laughed. "Did Ichabod say how she did it?"

"No, just that she'd had help from Ron. She was a Treacle."

Greg inhaled sharply. "That fucking bloke…"

"I know." George got up. "Right, I'm off to bed. I'm tired now."

"Oh, cheers, because I'm not."

George chuckled and walked out, leaving the door open to annoy him.

"Door, George!"

"What? If you're not tired, you can get up and shut it yourself."

"Wanker."

Grinning, George got into bed, staring at the ceiling. His mind had decided that sleep wasn't going to come just yet after all, and it swirled with not only Lil's story but this shit with Hailey. It wouldn't take much to question people as to who she was seeing, who that man was who'd been to her house earlier, but asking about him could get back to her, and they wanted her none the wiser that they knew what she was up to. They planned to follow the blondes after they'd been to The Angel tomorrow night, to where they planned to accost their target, then step in.

In case that was Kitchen Street, which had been mentioned at some point in the laundrette,

George would be having a word with the watchers who kept an eye on the sex workers, telling them to turn a blind eye to what was happening at the other end of the road. All the women would be told the same.

On the way home tonight, they'd driven down Kitchen to get their bearings. The streetlights down the far end were out, two houses boarded up, so that was a bonus. If that was where Hailey and her cohort planned to stab the fella, there was less chance of them being spotted by residents.

Ichabod had phoned in after he'd caught the suspected target at Hailey's, explaining what had been said, the whole street under The Brothers' protection. While it would have been a good bluff in other circumstances, there was now a risk that the man wouldn't turn up tomorrow night. Rather than bawl Ichabod out, George had kept his annoyance to himself — unusual for him — and prayed the target was arrogant enough to go there anyway, regardless.

What would his reason be for being on Kitchen, though? Yes, he'd 'changed his women', and maybe he was the peeper type who liked to observe from afar before approaching them, but why *else* would he be there? The watchers hadn't said about anything going on down that end recently, so it was a bit of a mystery.

Not knowing all the ins and outs always pissed George off, he craved control, but this was one time where he had to keep his mouth shut. They couldn't poke around and risk alerting him that something was up, so for now, George would have to remain in the dark.

Chapter Eight

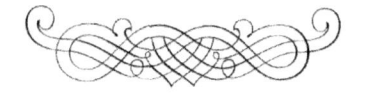

Bryan Flint hated Joe with a passion. But he hated the twins more. Being told to work for them had riled him up, but he hadn't been able to say no. Some PI of theirs, one he'd dubbed Nosy Parker, had videoed him being a bastard to Joe and extorting money out of him. That was enough to get Flint the sack, but George had shown him other damning evidence which meant Flint had no choice but to work for them.

He had to admit, the proposed pay was bloody decent. Cash in hand was always good, he never turned down readies, but what he had to do for it… Could he handle snooping on the police database, skewing investigations? The latter, not really. He wasn't on the murder squad, Janine Sheldon led that team, so if people went missing or turned up dead, how was he supposed to cover shit up for them? He'd tried to explain how it worked, how he'd be seen as suss, but those fucking bastards weren't having any of it.

"Make it work, that's what you'll be getting paid for. And maybe we can get you moved to the murder squad."

"How?"

"None of your business."

Did they have another copper on their books who could make that happen? At work, Flint would be conscious of how he was behaving even more than he already was. The others in his team thought he was a bang-up bloke, happy to help anyone, and it was hard keeping up that façade. Now, there was even more pressure, and that was why he'd been following Joe around tonight and had a chat with him at the trap house. He'd needed to feel in control again, top dog instead of someone lower down the ladder. Thanks to the twins, some of the shine had been buffed off his life.

He'd left the trap house and stood in the front garden for ages amongst the tall weeds and grass that had overgrown during the summer. Contemplated going down the other end and snagging a woman.

Fuck it. He'd go and see if anyone took his fancy near The Roxy. The sex workers were all too old for him. He reckoned they were in their twenties.

He walked with his head down and hood up, hands in pockets, well aware how difficult it was for the police to get a proper gander at a suspect's face on CCTV when they did that. He'd opted for dark clothing—the amount of criminals who gave themselves away with distinctive ticks or stripes on their trainers, or logos on their tops, was ridiculous. This outfit was far removed from his workday suit, and because he was so amenable at the station, no one would imagine for one minute what he got up to, so if he was caught on screen, his name would never enter their heads.

He sauntered into the street from the bottom end so he avoided passing the working girls and watchers. By The Angel, he swivelled his face to the right so the bloke in the alley over the road couldn't get a bead on him. He prepared himself to have to enter The Roxy, to be caught on camera, but as luck would have it, a drunk woman stumbled out of the nightclub, heading to Debbie's Corner.

Fucking hell.

Flint kept going as if he wasn't anyone to be worried about. He passed the sex workers, head down again, casually loping along like a teenager, the way so many of them did, as if they had a weird limp. The woman from The Roxy turned right, so he followed slowly until he was no longer visible from the corner.

"Are you all right, love?" he called.

She glanced over her shoulder, then walked faster.

"You shouldn't be out here alone."

"Fuck off," she snapped, not weaving now, as if him speaking to her had stripped the drunkenness right out of her. Adrenaline had a habit of sobering you up.

"Seriously, I'm not a weirdo. I just want you to get home safe."

Something in his voice must have come across as sincere, because she stopped. Spun round. He moved his hood back a little so she could see his face. Smiled.

"All right, so you don't *look* like a pervert..." She laughed.

Oh, you have no idea... "I'm a police officer, actually." He fished in his pocket for his fake ID and held it up for her. He'd be stupid to show her the real one, she'd see his name. This one, John Stokes, was about as bland as you could get.

She squinted at it. "Okay, John, what are you doing following women at night? *That's* not too creepy, is it?"

"I've just finished work, hence this getup." He gestured to his clothes. "I'm on my way back to my car after surveilling someone."

"Where is it?"

"Chancer's Lane." He'd sat in it for ages earlier, waiting for Joe to come out of his flat, then went after him on foot. The pleb hadn't even noticed.

She tugged her bag strap farther up her shoulder. "Oh, I'm near there, so we may as well walk together."

She looped her arm with his, and he tucked the ID away. If he'd judged right, she was in her early twenties but looked much younger, just the way he liked them. He preferred teens, they were easier to manipulate and threaten, but this one would do for tonight. She'd scratch an itch. She chattered on about her evening, how she'd stormed out of The Roxy because her friend had pissed her off, and he made all the right noises.

She switched topics abruptly. "So is it good being a copper?"

"It pays the bills."

"Do you get to use a Taser an' that?"

"Sometimes."

"You're really nice, you are. I don't normally like pigs."

"Some can be arseholes, I'll give you that. Lucky for you, I'm not one of them. Here's my car, but I'd rather see you to your door first." It wasn't his vehicle, but she wasn't to know that.

"Don't blame me if my dad comes out to bombard you with twenty questions by the way.

He does my nut in whenever a bloke walks me back. Embarrassing sod."

Shit, he'd assumed she'd have her own place.

He grinned to hide his annoyance, his stupidity in not asking her whether she had a housemate so he knew whether she was a safe bet or not. "If we're quiet, he won't know I'm there, then you won't have to be embarrassed, will you."

"Oh, he'll know, trust me."

They continued on, although Flint had lost the urge of the hunt now he couldn't get what he wanted. His shoulders slumped with defeat. They entered the next street, and she opened the gate to number two.

The front door flew open, and a man in a white T-shirt stared at him. "What's your game? Don't even think about coming in here and banging my daughter. You're old enough to be her bloody father!"

"Dad!"

Flint took his fake ID out of his pocket and held it up. They were too far apart for the bloke to see the name, but if he wanted to come forward to check, Flint was all for it. "I'd just finished a job and saw her leaving The Roxy by herself, so I walked her home. You can't be too careful these days."

"Ah. Right. I appreciate that." Dad moved aside to let his daughter in. "What have I bloody told you about being outside on your own at night, Alice?"

"Yeah, yeah."

A roll of the eyes showed the man's exasperation. He faced Flint again. "Thanks, you know, for getting her back safe."

"Not a problem. Night." Flint walked away, cursing a blue streak under his breath.

He usually picked young girls up online on a group called London Teens, using a different username each time, posing as a kid. He got chatting to them, gaining their trust, their phone numbers, addresses, then eventually getting nude pictures. He sold them on to eager perverts, made a tidy sum from it, then blackmailed the girls into leaving small amounts of cash in a coloured envelope in a specific location—small, because he couldn't expect them to find grands. The thrill of picking that up, of being caught, always got him hard. He was playing a fucking dodgy game but couldn't seem to help it.

Now he worked for the twins, he'd told himself he'd pack that in, the younger ones, go for those who were over eighteen. Stop blackmailing them but get pictures he could flog for five hundred quid each to deviants on the web.

Thank God Nosy Parker wasn't the type to break into Flint's flat and poke around on his perv laptop. If he had, there would have been no job offer, just a knife slice to the throat for being a nonce.

Get your shit together. Everything's changed now. This is not *a game.*

Shame his greed didn't get the memo.

Chapter Nine

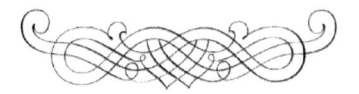

Pete had sunk a skinful in the Red Lion and had trouble seeing straight. He ordered a basket of chips to soak the booze up, and while he waited, sat on a stool at the bar and prayed he didn't fall off. Amy had really pissed him off earlier at her parents' house when they'd been round there for dinner, and he'd had to leave her and Joe there because he couldn't wallop her

in front of them. His anger had been too much to hide, so the Red Lion it was.

The in-laws thought he was the perfect husband, and he didn't want them seeing he wasn't. He'd learned this game as a kid from watching his best mate's dad manipulate his wife. It had fascinated him, how the woman had obeyed, how she'd flinched and cowered, and he'd vowed to treat his own woman like that when he eventually got one. He'd also adopted the shape thing. He liked the way each family member had one, which showed where they were in the pecking order. Pete had chosen a star, like his mate's dad, because he was *a fucking star, top of the Christmas tree.*

He glanced around. There were two knobheads in tonight, the sort of twats who thought they were above everyone else. The ones who put suits on for work and carried briefcases, acting like their office jobs were more meaningful than his, as though doing manual labour somehow made you inferior. Mind you, they must go to the gym, because they were packing some muscle.

"Tarquin feels Chandler needs to up his game on the stock market," the black-haired one said, all plum-in-the-mouth toff. He twiddled a moustache that

belonged on the face of a mac-wearing pervert. "He lost half a mil for the Taylors today."

"I heard about that. A mere drop in the ocean for that account, they're loaded, but really, what a doofus." The blond guffawed—an actual fucking guffaw—and he stroked an immaculate short beard with a point on the end.

They reminded Pete of those fuckers in Shakespearean times or something, especially the blond fella.

He glared at them.

The black-haired man caught him looking and cocked his head. "Do you have a problem, sir?"

Sir? The man either thought Pete was old, calling him that, or he was taking the piss somehow, although he couldn't work out how 'sir' being used was a joke— he'd had too much to drink but knew a slur when he heard one. It got to him, and he clenched his fists, getting himself prepared for a confrontation.

"Yeah, I do as it happens." He got off the stool and puffed his chest out. "People like you don't belong in here with the working class." He gestured around at all those in 'normal' clothes, their hands full of calluses, their broken nails, their skin weathered from being out in the sun doing back-breaking work.

"I rather thought an establishment like this admitted anyone who's willing to pay for a beverage."

Establishment? Beverage? Why couldn't they speak proper English?

"You stick out like a sore thumb," Pete said.

"One rather likes that," Perv-in-a-Mac said to his friend. "It would be dreadful to fade into the wallpaper, don't you think?"

Shakespeare nodded. "To be seen in a crowd is to arrive."

Pete couldn't make head nor tail of that, it sounded like some poetic bollocks. "Why don't you just fuck off and do one?"

"Do one?" Perv-in-a-Mac repeated. "I'm not quite sure what that means. Is it some kind of special language only the lower class know?"

That got Pete riled up. "Who are you calling lower class? I said us lot are working *class, you fucking div."*

Shakespeare waved that away. "All the same to us. Rabble. Uneducated."

He never did just say that. *"So why come here then if we're rabble?"*

Pete looked around for support, but it seemed no one else wanted to get involved. Typical. Whenever they'd *had rows, he'd jumped up and punched a few people's lights out, even got the boot in, but it was obvious they weren't about to return the bastard favour.*

"*Sit down, Pete,*" *Ian Holmes called over.* "*You've had enough.*"

"*Don't tell me when you think I've had enough. I'm the only one who knows that.*" *He* had *had enough, else he wouldn't have bought the fucking chips to soak the booze up, which, incidentally, hadn't arrived yet. Another thing to piss him off.* "*Where's my basket of chips? The bloody service in here's gone to the dogs.*"

"*Like Ian said, you've had enough.*" *Dave, the landlord, came over to take Pete's elbow.*

"*Get your manky paw off me.*"

Dave raised his eyebrows. "*Do you want to be barred?*"

That penetrated Pete's brain. This was his local, where he came to think up things to do to Amy, nasty things that gave him pleasure, and where he drank with his mates, although really they were just blokes, they weren't friends in the true sense. Still, they spoke to him, didn't they? That counted for something.

"*All right, I'll eat my chips then go.*"

Dave turned. "*There they are, look, on the bar. There's even a bottle of brown sauce because we know you like that. Now sit down and behave.*"

Pete enjoyed a bit of brown, although the brand he liked had taken to adding salt to it. Amy swore blind it was exactly the same as before, though. If Joe hadn't agreed with her, Pete would say she'd put it in there. He glanced at the bottle, a different one to at home, and ambled over to his stool, giving the toffs a mean glare while he was at it.

The chips were too hot, and he burnt his mouth. Something else to naff him off.

"We should be going soon," Perv-in-a-Mac said. "It smells of scum in here, plus Jessica's asked me not to make it a late one."

Scum? Was that directed at me?

"Then she needs telling she can't call the shots," Pete answered, his mouth full of chips. "She should be taught her place."

Shakespeare laughed at him. "This isn't the fifties. Women have equal rights and should be treated the same as men. Good Lord, sir, get with the programme."

Pete gritted his teeth. "Call me 'sir' one more time…"

Perv-in-a-Mac chortled. "Oh, I think you've rattled his cage."

I'll rattle something in a minute. Your fucking neck.

Pete chomped on more chips, entertaining thoughts of following these two wankers outside and giving them a thump or ten. He'd knock them out easily, despite their muscles, and even if he didn't, he'd have had a good bleedin' go. Any excess anger he could take out on Amy when he got home. She'd be waiting for it anyway because of earlier.

The toffs had about two mouthfuls of their lagers left, so Pete rammed more chips down his throat, annoyed with himself for forgetting to squeeze brown sauce all over them. He hadn't put salt and vinegar on either, and his anger levels rose, as did his blood pressure. He really needed to get that seen to, but he didn't do doctors.

Perv-in-a-Mac finished his pint and placed the glass on the bar. Pete eyed it, dying to pick it up, smash the edge, and spear the cunt's face with the spiky bits. Dave seemed to twig what he was contemplating and wagged a finger. It bugged Pete, being told what to do, but if he wanted to continue drinking here, he'd have to behave.

Shakespeare added his glass to the bar, leaving lager dregs. "Shall we tootle off then, old chap?"

Jesus wept, they really were too posh for words. Pete shook his head at the unfairness, how some were born with silver spoons in their gobs yet others had plastic, too many with no spoon at all. He tutted, watching the men head for the door.

"I've had enough, you're right," he said to Ian. "I'm off home."

"Right at the same time as those two?" Ian tutted. "They're brick shithouses, mate, look like they box in their spare time, so good luck."

"They're no problem."

"There's two of them and one of you. You're going to get hurt."

"Nah, it'll be them going home with broken legs, you'll see."

Ian laughed. "How many have you had?"

"What are you getting at?"

"You know we get beer goggles, yeah?"

"Yeah…"

"The same applies to fights. Booze makes us see things differently. We think we're Mike Tyson when we're actually bantamweights."

"Knob off." Pete left, and on the pavement, he glanced left to right. Fucking hell! Talking to Ian meant the men had got away. He stomped down the road, past some shuttered shops, then rounded the corner, heading for home. "Bantamweights. What is he on?"

He continued, coming to the end of the street where the tarts stood touting for business. He stopped and eyed up a brunette. She reminded him of Amy when she used to look good and, overindulgence of alcohol aside, his dick stirred.

"How much?" he asked.

She eyed him up and down and laughed. "You've got to be kidding me."

"Eh?"

"The state of you, and I'm not just talking about being drunk. Beer gut, ugly, bad breath…I could go on. Thanks but no thanks."

Anger boiled so quickly Pete almost didn't stop himself from launching a right hook at her smug-bitch face. Cheeky slag. Who the fuck did she think she was talking to? Others tittered—he hated the way women did that, witches round their cauldron—and he balled his hands into fists.

"If you're thinking of using those on me, think again," Amy-but-not-Amy said. "I've got a black belt in karate, so fuck the hell off."

He believed her, she looked the type to have a mean kick on her.

"Watch your mouth in future," he barked and walked on, fuming, thinking up ways he could snatch

her one night and rape her down an alley. That'd teach her to have a smart mouth.

Time skipped, and he found himself on Kitchen Street. He weaved down it towards more dirty slappers, foregoing speaking to any of them in case there was a repeat of his last encounter. There was only so much humiliation he could take in one night, and it had started with those bloody toffs.

Was he losing his touch, his air of menace?

He dipped down a cut-through street, then into an alley that would come out near Blanchard Crescent where he lived—well, a street away. It was a long, thin stretch of darkness, and he upped his pace a bit. While he wasn't scared of anyone, he still needed to be careful. Kids sold drugs round here, and any of them could gang up on him—or try to.

Halfway down, footsteps thudded behind him, so he walked faster. If he could get to the end where a streetlamp was, he could see who it was when they came out. He knew people who lived in a couple of the houses there, so he could shout for reinforcements if necessary.

He sensed two sets of feet and told himself it was a bloke and his missus on their way home, seeing as no one had called out to him or gripped his jacket from behind. Relaxing, he popped out at the end, turned right, and stopped beneath a lamppost. Waited.

The toffs emerged.

"Well, what do you know," Pete said. "Posh Spice one and two, except she's way better-looking than you two."

Shakespeare smiled. "Just the man we wanted to see."

Where had his hoity-toity accent gone?

Pete frowned. "What's your fucking game?"

Perv-in-a-Mac swung his briefcase to and fro beside him. "I'd shut your mouth if I were you."

"Or what?" Pete broadened his shoulders and bowed his arms, fists ready to fly.

The briefcase came up quicker than he could process it, slamming into the side of his head. Fuck, what did it have in it to be so heavy? He staggered to the right, tripping down the kerb, twisting his ankle and going down to one knee in the road. Jesus, his head hurt from that wallop. Another clout landed, sending him to his back on the tarmac. They kicked him, their pointed shoes undoubtedly capped with steel under that shiny leather. He covered his head with his hands, his face as best he could using his forearms. Received the pasting of his life, each kick agony, and he swore a couple of ribs cracked. He made the mistake of moving a hand to lay it on his side, and a shoe tip crash-landed on his face, splitting his top lip, one of his teeth coming loose.

Unable to defend himself—the onslaught was too fast and violent, too brutal—he gave in and let them think he was dead. He went limp, closing his eyes, and at last, the hits stopped.

"Check if he's breathing," one of them said.

Pete couldn't work out who it was now they weren't speaking posh.

"If he is, suffocate the bastard."

Hold up! What *did he just say?*

Pete opened his eyes and tried to get up, desperate now to save his life, but the sole of Perv-in-a-Mac's shoe planted on his face and pushed him back down.

"Listen to me, you fucking arsemonger." Pure East End, no Chelsea about him, darling. "This is the last lesson you'll ever learn, but before you go, know that certain people have friends who'll help them. You're not as all-powerful as you think." He wrenched Pete up to sitting, then swung his briefcase into his face.

Pete flew backwards with the force, his nose breaking, hot blood gushing over his lips. He groaned and rolled onto his side, then purposely shallow-breathed. Closed his eyes. He sensed them either crouching by him or bending to have a good gander, so he held his breath for what seemed like forever.

Something touched his neck—fingers?—then Not-From-Chelsea said:

"Dead. Job done."

"Thank God for that. Carrying a briefcase with a fucking breeze block in it isn't my idea of fun." That must be Shakespeare.

"Killing him was, though."

"Are we leaving him there?"

"Nah, we'll drag him to the alley where it's dark."

Pete couldn't hold his breath any longer and, once they took hold of him, he let it out while they were distracted, then breathed in through his mouth, his nose too clogged with blood to let any air in. Held by his arms and ankles, he swayed, then the motion of being let go and thrown almost brought up his chips. He thudded onto the ground and waited for a long time before he opened his eyes.

They'd gone.

He tried to move, but his body had seized up on him. He shut his eyes, just for a bit, until he had the energy to force himself upright. A little sleep wouldn't hurt.

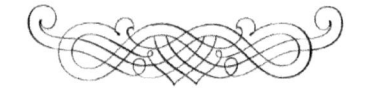

Chapter Ten

For two hours, Hailey had listened to Delaney chortling on about going to Ken and Polly's.

His excitement was usually infectious, and she loved the fact he had two other people in his life who adored him so much, but today she couldn't muster up any true enthusiasm. So she faked it, guilt prodding her because she couldn't wait for him to leave. So he was safe.

A triple knock had her jumping, and she chased after Delaney who ran down the hallway, trying to reach up and open the door.

"No, you've been told about that. Mummy must answer it."

He danced in place to the side of her, irritatingly chanting, "Nanny, Nanny, Nanny."

Poor sod, it wasn't his fault she was so on edge, but God!

Hailey peered into the peephole. Ken looked weird through the fisheye lens, his nose, lips, and chin too prominent, his eyes recessed. Door open, she stepped back to allow Delaney to do his usual: throwing himself at Polly's legs and gripping tight.

"Oh my word, someone's pleased to see us," Ken said. "You'd think we'd been away for years!" He smiled at Hailey. "Do you mind if we don't nip in for a cuppa, love? We've got a day out planned." He winked, maybe to stop Hailey from protesting that they spoiled her son.

"Fine by me," she said to ease any of his worries on that score. She glanced over his shoulder. A different man sat in the same car as last night. Her stomach rolled, but she hid her unease. "You can spoil him rotten for all I care. Be good, Delaney."

"I will."

"See you soon," Polly said.

Delaney skipped along beside her as she led him to their car.

"Are you okay?" Ken asked. "You look a bit pale."

Hailey loved the way Ken treated her like a daughter. He was the father figure she'd never had. "Just tired."

"I'm not surprised. He's a handful, isn't he. I've said it before, but you're a marvel, bringing him up on your own. If you want us to have him once a month instead of every six weeks to give you more of a break, just say so, all right? We love having him. It's like watching Riley grow up all over again." Sadness took over his face, and he sighed. "Still, no point dwelling on things. He's not coming back, so we have to make the best of it, don't we."

"Sadly, yes." A day didn't go by where she hadn't cursed that little bastard who'd mown Riley down. The fact he was in prison didn't ease her grief any.

Ken reached out and touched her arm. How she didn't break down crying she didn't know. He was so like Riley, just older, and sometimes it hurt to look at him.

"We're here if you need us," he said. "Before I forget, we were wondering if we could take the little man away with us this summer. Spain. The hotel we just stayed at has so much for kids to do, and I think he'd love it. You're welcome to come, too, of course."

"That's very kind of you, but you can have him to yourself, I don't mind."

"Brilliant. Right, well, we'd best be off. Sealife then the cinema. He'll like that."

She wished she was going with them.

Ken strode away, and Hailey waited for them to drive past so she could do the obligatory wave. Delaney's little face pressed to the window at the back, him kissing the glass as if he kissed her, and a horrible whoosh of emotions overtook her. What if that was the last time she got to see him as a free woman?

She closed the door, leaning against it, and closed her eyes. Hot tears fell, and she asked herself if this was the way to go—killing Joe without any help other than Stacey's. They didn't know what they were doing, not really, and she was sure they hadn't factored everything in. A niggle at the back of her mind, one she couldn't pin down, convinced her they'd forgotten something. And seeing Delaney just now…it brought home exactly what she'd be giving up if she was in prison. Her rage towards Joe shouldn't outweigh seeing her son grow up.

She turned, double-locked the door, put the chain across, and went into the living room. Even though she planned to go out in a sec, she didn't trust that Joe wouldn't come in during the couple of minutes she left the door unlocked. She slid her hand under the sofa and felt along the carpet for the burner phone. This could be a case of getting cold feet, but a nasty feeling inside her whispered that the plan would go wrong, they'd be caught. She *had* to listen to her instincts.

She dropped the phone in her cardigan pocket and went to put her shoes and coat on. Thankfully, she never worked Saturdays, her assistant manager held the fort, so she was free to go off and use the phone. She left via the back door, locking it behind her, and took cash out of her tin in the shed. She walked down the alley at the rear of the houses, coming out in another street and boarding a bus that had just drawn up. She got off at King's Cross, losing herself amongst the travellers at the train station. Upstairs, she bought a coffee, sausage roll, and a ring doughnut from Greggs, sitting at a table overlooking the commuters who stood in a crowd staring at the arrivals and departure boards like trained zombies.

Burner in hand, she messaged Stacey before she chickened out. It didn't matter whether Stacey agreed with her decision or not—she didn't have a child to think about.

H: I'VE CHANGED MY MIND. I'M GOING TO TELL THE BROTHERS INSTEAD.

S: THANK GOD FOR THAT. NOW IT'S COME TO IT, I WOKE UP THIS MORNING SHITTING MYSELF. I WAS BEING SO BRAVE UP UNTIL THEN, TOO!

H: DO YOU WANT THEM TO KNOW HE HURT YOU?

S: OOH, I MIGHT GET COMPENSATION OFF THEM. LOL. ONLY JOKING. IF IT MEANS HE GETS PUNISHED MORE, THEN YES, ALTHOUGH I DON'T WANT THEM COMING TO MINE OR ANYTHING. I HAVEN'T TOLD MY FELLA WHAT JOE DID YET. CAN'T FACE IT. IF THEY WANT TO TALK TO ME, WE'LL HAVE TO ARRANGE TO MEET SOMEWHERE ELSE.

H: OKAY, WILL KEEP YOU POSTED IF YOU WANT?

S: Yes. Now there's no reason why we can't get caught texting each other, are you okay with me putting your number in my normal phone?

H: Yep.

S: Good luck!

But even if The Brothers killed Joe, wouldn't Hailey and Stacey still be suspects once the police found out they'd both been his girlfriend? Wasn't it still sensible not to contact one another on their regular mobiles? Maybe they could say they knew each other from before Joe. They were friends. But that wouldn't explain why they'd only just started texting.

Shaking now she'd made the final decision, because approaching The Brothers was a daunting prospect, Hailey popped the burner in her pocket, her other phone bleeping. She took it out and checked the message: Boo! It's meeee, Staceeeeey!

Hailey added the number to her contacts, replying: Yoo hoo!

Would they become friends now? Hailey had distanced herself from hers—Joe didn't like them—only replying to their messages every now and then so she didn't look a complete cow, until they'd eventually tapered off contacting her altogether. She didn't feel she could randomly pop back into their lives full force, she'd seem like a user, plus they'd already think she'd ghosted them and might not be receptive. Maybe Stacey was the way to go, a new start, and they already had so much in common, even if it *was* abuse from Joe.

She ate her sausage roll, thinking of ways to contact the twins. There wasn't a resident handbook that listed their phone number or any advice on how to get hold of them. But what if she spoke to that man sitting in her street? Maybe he could ring them, give them her number.

She moved on to the doughnut, going through everything in her head, what she'd say, what she'd ask them to do. Would she get in trouble for not telling them sooner that Joe ran a county line? She hadn't known for long, but would they punish her for keeping it to herself? No, surely not. She could say she was too scared of Joe to have come forward. It wasn't a lie, she was.

She finished her doughnut and sipped her coffee. Hours ago, she'd planned to willingly make herself a murderer, and now, what was she? An accessory? What was it called when you asked men to kill someone for you?

She took the burner out and switched it off. On her way towards the stairs, she slipped it in a bin wrapped in her paper bags from Greggs, then went down and headed to the toilets. She smiled at the queue of people waiting to have their photo taken at the brick wall, pretending they were on their way to wizard school. They seemed so excited, nothing pressing going on in their lives.

She envied them.

Toilet visit over, she stepped outside to catch the bus home, walking over to stand near Burger King. Traffic buzzed along, and people rushed towards King's Cross or St Pancreas, maybe the posh shopping area Hailey couldn't afford to spend money in. Those in suits, were they off to the Google building?

She spied a taxi, tempted to flag it down so she could go to Camden Market, pretend everything was okay for an hour or two, but no, she had more important things on her list, and wandering around there was only delaying the inevitable.

The bus arrived, and she hopped on, sitting on the very edge of a seat beside a smelly man, no other spaces available. He stank of BO, his nicotine-stained fingers strumming at his bottom lip. Despite that, she'd bet he was nicer than Joe.

Back in Princeton Avenue, she walked down the pavement dragging her feet, apprehension coiling in her gut. But it was better to hand this over than do it herself. Knowing her luck, as soon as she'd got the knife out to stab Joe, she'd crap herself, and he'd laugh, calling her a stupid weak slag.

She crossed the road and approached the car, sidestepping to the driver's window. The man inside raised his eyebrows at her, gesturing for her to go round the other side and get in. She shook her head, so he lowered the window.

"Are you…can you phone The Brothers for me?"

"What for, love?"

"I'm…I need help."

"Hailey, isn't it?"

Him knowing her name sent a bolt of fear through her, but of *course* he'd know it if the twins had taken over the street. She didn't imagine they wouldn't have poked into everyone who lived here.

Apprehension raged in her chest. "Um, yes."

"I'll just message them for you. Hang on."

He prodded his phone, and she glanced up and down the road, expecting Joe to pop up and run at her, whisking her home to beat her up. She worried Mum would nose out of her living room window and see her, come out and ask what was going on, but she remembered it was her turn to do a Saturday at the play centre.

"They said to meet them at The Angel," the bloke said. "Want a lift?"

"No, thank you. I'll walk."

"Are you sure? I mean, is that wise, considering that man who bothered you last night, plus what you plan to do tonight?"

Oh my fucking God, they know! Who told them?

"I don't know what you mean," she said.

"Look, do you want me to give them a bell so they can tell you I'm kosher? I'm not in the habit of taking women off in my car unless the twins tell me to, so there's no need to worry, but I understand why you'd be cautious. You don't know me from Adam."

"Go on then."

He poked at his screen, and FaceTime launched. George's face appeared—or was it Greg's?—and the driver said, "She doesn't want a lift for obvious reasons, but I don't want her out on her own. Can you tell her I'm safe?" He swung the phone around.

The twin smiled at her. "Come to your senses, have you?"

She frowned. "What are you on about?"

"By speaking to us."

"Um…yes?"

"Good. Sensible. Get in the motor with Martin. He's fucking harmless. I mean, look at him. Does he seem the type to get up to anything dodgy?"

She didn't say that *anyone* could be dodgy, regardless of what they looked like. Instead, she shook her head and walked round to the passenger side, hoping Mum's nosy next-door neighbour wasn't getting an eyeful of her climbing into a stranger's car. She put her seat belt on, and Martin popped the phone in the cup holder then put his window up. He peeled away from the kerb.

"Do the twins own the street now?" she asked for something to say.

"No. Are you referring to you being under their protection?"

"Yes."

"That's just something our man told the bloke who was at your door last night. To get him off your back."

"How come the twins know what I was going to do? I didn't tell anyone other than…than my friend."

"Let's just say some people have flapping ears and leave it at that."

"The man from the laundrette. He was the one who told…who told my visitor to go away."

Martin glanced across and smiled at her. "The twins will explain. You're doing the right thing, you know. They'll help you. They helped me, and my life's never been the same since. I owe them everything."

"What did they do?"

"Rescued me."

"What from?"

He shrugged. "That's in the past, something I prefer not to think about. Anyway, you've got your own shit to concentrate on."

"Sorry for being nosy."

"It's all right."

He pulled in down the side of The Angel and parked. They got out at the same time, and she checked the street, then fretted Joe might be inside.

What if he was and he caused a scene?

Chapter Eleven

In Debbie's old room at the parlour in The Angel, George assessed Hailey. She sat on the sofa, twiddling her shaking fingers and staring everywhere but at him, Greg, and Ichabod. A cornered rabbit? Was she hiding something and worried they'd get it out of her? What, exactly, was her game?

His back was up because he didn't know *why* she wanted to kill that fella. No one decided to murder someone on their Estate without permission and got away with it. She was lucky they were prepared to step in and take over, providing the bloke deserved it, but if he found out she was playing them, lying about her reasons…

If she does, she'll get the sharp edge of my tongue. I'll cut her to fucking pieces.

Lil had said both blondes were at the far end of their twenties, but their PI, Mason, had done some digging last night and told them how old Hailey was. Twenty-one, and she *did* look older, but only because she seemed to have lived a hard life. She had that vibe about her. Worn out. Barely holding it together. Had Noelle struggled to bring her up as a single parent? Had Hailey suffered hardships, the proof of which now lived on her face in the form of wrinkles she shouldn't have yet? Some people had it tough, and you could just tell.

Was she one of those rough-and-ready types, gearing herself up to give them a load of verbal, despite coming forward for help? Those sorts of people got right up his nose. Bolshy, entitled. He still hadn't got her measure visually, so he'd test the waters by inspecting her responses.

"First off, tell us who that wanker is, the one you intended to kill." He caught her tensing. Didn't she like authority? Tough tits, because he and Greg were the authority around here, and she'd do well to remember that. "Look, the sooner we know, the sooner we can get Ichabod to follow him around today. You were going after him tonight, but we could grab him earlier, see? Get things sorted quicker so your mind's put at rest. That's what you want, isn't it?"

"Joe Osbourne. Joseph, but he hates being called that."

Good, then that's what I'll address him as. Wind the fucker up. "And where does he live?"

"Chancer's Lane."

"I see by your little smile you think it's appropriate he lives there. *Is* he a chancer?"

"I didn't used to think he was."

Ichabod left the room to sort the necessary: contacting Mason to do a search. Flint was having today off from his police job, time he'd been taking here and there because he had annual leave stacked up. Besides, Flint hadn't had his initiation yet. Since they'd visited him to inform him he'd be working for them, they'd left him alone on purpose. To stew. Worry. Wonder when the first message would come through.

"Where's Joe likely to hang around today?"

Hailey shrugged. "He could be anywhere. I thought I knew him but… He told me he was a carpenter, but I found out he wasn't. A few days ago. I haven't known long."

George sensed she was scared and hadn't come here to fuck them over. He softened his tone a bit. "Regardless of your part in this, and we'll get to that shortly, if you want to kill Joseph, then he must have done something bad to you. We'll get rid of him if we deem it necessary, but you have to tell us why he deserves to die. We're not in the habit of bumping people off just on someone's say-so." He'd test her. "Or are *you* the bad one? You and your mate, and you need to get rid of him because he knows about something you've done?"

Her head shot up. "No!"

"So you believe he needs to be sorted, you're not just a mad pair of bints doing it for kicks?"

Her face flickered with spite. "That man—if he can even be called a man—deserves everything he gets after what he's done to us." She shoved the sleeve of her coat up to reveal a scabby skewed square with a J in the middle.

"Ah, so he's a marker."

She frowned. "A what?"

"Someone who likes to brand people, so to speak. Make sure everyone knows they belong to him for whatever reason. So this could be significant: what is that around the letter, a diamond?"

"I thought it was a rhombus," she said. "Or a graffiti artist's 'O'."

"Rhombus, diamond, same thing really as shapes go," Greg said.

"Could this be his tag?" George asked her.

She seemed confused. "Tag?"

Fuck me sideways. Is she deliberately being thick or is her brain lagging because she's got too much in it? "Does he belong to a gang? That sort of tag."

"I... He must do."

"What do you mean, he must do?" God love her and everything, but she was seriously getting on his nips. "Listen to me." He sat opposite her instead of towering above, realising, too fucking late, that he didn't need to employ intimidation tactics with her. "If we're to help you, we need to know everything. Like I said, regardless of your part in it."

"But I didn't play a part!"

"So what are you fucking being *vague* for?" He cursed himself. "Sorry, love, but I'll be honest and say you're doing my nut in. Just tell me what's what. *Now*."

"He runs a county line," she blurted.

Anger surged, but George tucked it away for later in the warehouse. "Right, that wasn't so hard, was it? And you found out a few days ago."

"Yes."

"And you want to kill him because he provides drugs?"

"No."

"What then?"

"He *raped me*," she spat.

Oh fuck. Oh Jesus fuck. "Christ. If you'd have said earlier, I wouldn't have been so heavy-handed."

Greg gave him a glare: *You're putting the blame for your temper on her?*

George hadn't intended for it to come out that way, but he'd apologise nonetheless. "I'm sorry. I was an arsehole just then. What I *meant* to say was—"

"I know what you meant. It's okay."

"No, it isn't."

"I'm just...I'm still coping with it, and it's painful to talk about."

"When did he do this?"

"Last Friday."

"So we're clear, yesterday or the Friday before?"

"The one before."

The night she first went into the laundrette. "Why the hell did he do it, do you know?"

Another Greg glare: *Are you implying she must have done something to deserve being raped? Sort yourself out, bruv.*

"I apologise again," George said. "Who knows why men do that sort of shit."

Hailey shivered. "He got angry. He caught me packing a suitcase. When we first got together, he was round mine all the time, he was nice, then he started being moody and leaving days in between visits, barely coming, so I thought he was seeing someone else. I asked around. Found out about the line from some bloke, that he'd lied to me, and he'd been sleeping with women, paying them for it."

"Who was the bloke?"

"I don't know, but he was in his forties, something like that. He knew a lot about Joe and warned me to keep away from him else I'd go down with him. He was in the Red Lion when I was asking questions, drunk, and he said he'd been watching Joe for a while."

"Have you ever seen that man before?"

"I don't think so."

"Back to the suitcase. Where were you going?"

"Wales, to see my aunt, to keep me and my son out of the way while you… I'd planned to tell you then go, but things changed."

"How?"

She laughed unsteadily, one of those laughs full of wryness, or perhaps it was disbelief. "If I believed in fate or the universe putting two people in the same place at the same time for a reason, that night would be one of those times."

George wished she'd just get on with it, say what she really had to say, but now he'd got her talking, he mustn't fuck this up. He had to remember she'd been violated and was vulnerable. "Go on."

"After…after he did what he did, on my little boy's bed—"

"You *what*?" Mad George pushed forward, the nutty-as-a-fruitcake alter who wanted to rip this Joseph cunt limb from limb.

"George…" Greg warned. "Rein him in. Let her finish before you allow Mad to go off on one." He smiled at Hailey. "He's not arsey at you, I promise."

"Who's Mad?" she whispered.

George had no problem owing his personas these days. "Some bloke I turn into when things boil my piss. Think of the Hulk."

"Right." A faint smile touched her lips. "Shall I carry on?"

"Yeah." George formed a double fist and squeezed.

"So, he'd cut my wrist, shoved me on the bed. Did what he wanted. There was blood on the quilt, his *stuff* because he hadn't used a condom, and he left, and the only thing I could focus on was buying a new duvet. I couldn't let Delaney sleep under that one, and if I went to the shops, it would take my mind off…off…" Her breathing hitched.

"I get it. What happened next?"

"My mum had Delaney overnight, so I ran to town. Went into Home Bargains. And Stacey was there."

"Who's that, the other blonde bird?"

"Yes. I knew who she was and didn't want to engage. She's Joe's ex. But she saw the cuts on my wrist, and she knew. Said Joe's name straight away. She showed me *her* wrist. She's got a tattoo and said her scar's under it."

George nodded. "Like I said, he's a marker. Right. So I take it you bought the quilt."

"She bought it for me. I nearly cried because she was so kind. And she bought one for herself, said she's doing up her spare room."

The one thing that had bugged Lil that first Friday night in the laundrette was that Hailey and Stacey had opened the packaging on brand-new quilts and washed them. It hadn't made sense to her, nor to George, so at least he'd be able to solve that conundrum and Lil could sleep easy at night.

He laughed internally at his own sarcasm. "You washed the quilts, we're aware of that. Why?"

"Stacey doesn't like the smell of new ones. She'd had one on her bed, a new one, I mean, when Joe raped her."

Mad prodded at George again, desperate to come out. *Wait, you fucking tosser. I need you later, not now.* "To cut a long story short, you decided to kill him."

Hailey opened up and told them everything. It took all of George's will not to go out there and find the prick.

She finished with, "I was so angry I wasn't thinking straight. I thought stabbing him myself would help me get over it all, but when I saw Delaney going off with his nan and grandad this morning, I just couldn't go through with it."

"Who are they, Joe's parents?"

"No, he's not my boy's father, thank God. Delaney's dad is dead."

I knew it. She's had it tough. "Sorry to hear that. How did he die?"

"He got knocked over."

"Shit. Have you told Stacey you've changed your mind?"

"Yes, earlier."

"How did she take it?"

"She's relieved. She wants you to know what he did to her. Maybe meet up and discuss it if you need more ammo to go after Joe, but her boyfriend doesn't know, and she doesn't want him to either."

"What you've given us is enough, but if she wants to talk, fine."

"So you're going to do it?"

"Yes."

She sagged with relief. "Am I in trouble?"

"Eh?"

"Because I didn't tell you about the line straight away."

"Nah. You intended to, so that's what counts, and fear played a big part in you keeping it to yourself. You said Delaney's gone off with his grandparents. Where?"

"Kent. He won't be home until the day before he goes back to school."

"Good. This aunt in Wales. Wasn't she curious when you didn't turn up?"

"I said I'd had to change my plans, couldn't get time off work after all."

"What about your mum. Noelle, isn't it?"

Hailey appeared shocked that he knew her name, then resigned. "I suppose you had to look into me."

"Yep. Will she be a problem? Will she need protection from Joe?"

"No, she doesn't know anything. I kept it to myself. She's at work today anyway."

"Do you still want to kill him?"

"No, I want you to do it, that's why I'm here."

George smiled. "What I mean is, do you want us to round him up and *let* you kill him? Are you angry enough to see it through? Or even cut him a bit, like he cut you? Mark the wanker?"

She nodded. "But I'm scared."

"I understand. Get hold of Stacey, tell her to come here, round the back. We'll have a chat, see if she wants to join in an' all. If not, she needs a word in her ear about keeping her trap shut about this."

Hailey took her phone out and typed a message.

"While we wait, fancy a drink?" George stood. "What's your poison?"

She looked up at him. "Bacardi and Coke. A bloody large one."

Chapter Twelve

Joe had been out all evening with his gang, so Amy had spent a few hours with Belinda, Roger grumping that she was there, encroaching on his alone time with his wife. Belinda had told him to shut his trap, and they'd talked in the kitchen with the door closed. At half past eleven, when Pete should have been home, Amy had gone to her house, checked Joe was in bed, then sat in the living room with yet another cuppa. She was dying to phone Lil, see if those men had done the job, but Lil had advised no contact out of the ordinary in case the police asked for Amy's mobile phone.

The idea of that scared her. In the past, there had been Google searches, her looking up undetectable causes of death. She had no excuse for them, and the police would come to the only natural conclusion. But Pete being beaten up would be classed as out of her control, unless they could prove she and Lil had conspired to make it happen. But the salt, that was another matter. She should have been more careful. Shit.

At four a.m. after dozing on and off, she went to bed, relief overtaking her that this had really happened, she'd got rid of him. She imagined her life of partial freedom — Joe was the remaining fly in the ointment — and thought about how she would live without being punched on the daily. If she avoided Joe as much as she could, it would be fine.

But a tinge of panic turned into a tsunami as she stared at the ceiling in the dark. Things roiled in her mind. The suspicion she might be under come tomorrow; viewing Pete's body to identify him and fake crying; the funeral to prepare for, fork out for;

applying for the life insurance, which was up to date because she paid for it out of her own bank, something she'd taken out years ago for just this moment; coping with Joe who'd go further off the rails with his father dead, sending her crazy in a different way.

She imagined her child getting so bad he turned to crime. Being arrested. Cautioned. Then he'd repeat offend and be taken to one of those youth detention centres, out of her hair. She'd visit him once a week for an hour, glad he wasn't at home anymore. And she'd paint over that fucking graffiti, erase all traces of him, because, in her daydream, he'd be sent away for years. By the time he got out, she'd tell him he was old enough to get a place of his own. Maybe she'd redecorate the whole house, do some of that up-cycling on the furniture, changing it to shabby chic or whatever. Dare she allow herself to become excited?

She glanced at the clock, the green numbers glowing. Pete had never stayed out this late unless he was going clubbing, stopping at the kebab van after—God, he still thought he was in his twenties, able to keep up with the best of them—so it was a given the men had done their job. She'd wanted to know who they were before they attacked Pete, see if she already knew them so she could deem them as trustworthy or not—it didn't sit right that they knew about her but she didn't know about them. She could be walking round town, oblivious if they strolled past her. But Lil had said no, the less Amy knew the better; she couldn't accidentally blurt anything to the police, then. It made sense, but it still bugged her.

She closed her eyes, exhaustion claiming her. She'd have to report him missing in a few hours. He never stayed out overnight, and because of that, if she didn't phone it in, it would look weird. Then she'd have to ring Lil, as planned, to say she couldn't go to work, what with the 'worry' of it all. Lil would say take all the time you need, and Amy would have to fret in front of any officers.

She could do that. Pretend.

After all, she'd been doing it for years.

The knock on the door razored a slice in her frazzled nerves, jitters bleeding out. Joe had left for school but must have forgotten something, plus his key if he hadn't let himself in, but then again, he'd find it amusing to pull her away from cleaning the hob to tend to his needs. He was his father all over.

She prepared herself for him to barge past her, knocking her against the wall, then opened the door ready to act subservient. Until she knew for sure Pete was dead, she'd behave as usual.

It wasn't Joe.

"Mrs Osbourne?" *a policeman in uniform asked.*

Another stood beside him, except it was a woman. Both had hats on, and she supposed that was as a sign of respect for the dead, their visit more official than the usual. She felt sorry for them, having to tell her the news, thinking she'd be upset, that her whole life had crashed down on her. She'd infected them with a part of her rotten world. Guilt bothered her over it, but she pushed it aside, geeing herself up to force tears and sobs out.

"Yes? Is it Pete?"

"Why would you ask that?"

"He didn't come home last night, and I was just about to ring you."

She blushed at the fact she had pink rubber gloves on and a scouring sponge in one hand, clear proof she hadn't been about to ring them at all. She'd made a mistake already. What if she fucked up again? What if they sensed she'd played a part in the murder? They were used to spotting liars, they saw so many of them. She'd have to find a point in the conversation where she could explain why she'd been cleaning when her husband was missing to cover her arse.

"Is it about him?" she pressed.

"I'm afraid so. Can we come in?"

They must have looked in Pete's wallet to know who he was, where to come. She could see it now, a copper fishing in his pocket to discover his name because his face was so fucked up he was unrecognisable.

"Oh no, it must be bad, then..." She stepped back, took her gloves off, and walked to the kitchen to lay them on the worktop, the sponge beside them. She turned, the coppers right there, *so imposing, and it startled her. "Do you...would like you a tea or coffee?"*

"Only if you're having one," the fella said.

Proud that he'd accepted—Mum said that if a workman or guest took a drink off you, they thought you were a clean person—Amy filled the kettle to halfway and clicked it on. She leaned her bum against one of the cupboards. "Is it bad news?"

"Why don't you sit down with me and let Sophie make the drinks. I'm Mike Allen, by the way."

Him asking her to sit was a big giveaway, and she walked over to the table and took a perch facing the officers. Mike sat opposite, blocking her view of Sophie taking cups out of the cupboard—cups that were in regimented lines beside equally regimented glasses, just the way Pete liked it. Would Sophie think Amy was weird for being so particular? If she didn't now, she would when she opened the cutlery drawer to look for a teaspoon.

Mike cleared his throat. "I'm sorry to bring you this news, but Pete was found in an alley this morning by someone on their way home from work."

"What was he doing there*?" Amy asked. "Oh God, did he get drunk and fall over? Knock himself out? Did he spend the night on the ground?"*

"We're not sure whether he was drunk yet, but yes, he slept on the pavement."

Slept? Did that mean the bastard was still alive?

Please, God, just do me this one favour...

"Poor thing." Amy clasped her hands together. "Is he okay? What on earth happened?"

"He's been taken to hospital. It appears he was attacked. Do you know where he went?"

"It would have been the Red Lion in town."

Mike spoke into his radio, passing on that information. He smiled at Amy. "Thank you for that, it'll be a big help. What time would he usually have been home?"

"No later than half eleven if he wasn't going on to The Roxy. By one o'clock, I assumed that's where he was and I fell asleep on the sofa."

"Why didn't you phone us when you woke up?"

"I thought Pete had come in and gone to bed, and as I'd spent the night on the sofa, I wouldn't have seen his side hadn't been slept in. I just got on with getting Joe off to school."

"Is that your son?"

Unfortunately, yes.

She nodded.

"So you didn't go upstairs to get dressed? You'd have seen the bed, then."

She'd muffed up again. *"No, I had a shower then took clothes from the clean pile over there."* She pointed to a washing basket on the floor in the corner, glad she hadn't put it away like she usually would. *"I did some cleaning, like I always do before work, thinking Pete would have already gone to his job, and in the middle of scrubbing the cooker, I went up to check he hadn't overslept or choked on vomit in his sleep or something. You know those horrible thoughts you get?"* Ones where you hope he *has* choked and all your worries are over? *"But he wasn't there, and the bed was made—he never makes it—so I knew then he hadn't come home. I came flying down to ring the police, then you knocked."*

"I see. Do you know of anyone who'd want to hurt him? The injuries are quite extensive."

She imagined his face obliterated by knife slashes and fought off a smile. "No. How bad is it?"

"He was unconscious when he was loaded into the ambulance."

"Oh God..." *She shook her head.* "He can be a bit volatile, likes to put his point of view across when he's had a drink." *That was a nice way of putting it.* "Maybe he had a row with someone in the pub and they followed him?"

"It's possible."

"Can I go and see him?"

"Yes." *Mike passed on which hospital Pete had been taken to.* "Is everything all right at home?"

Here we go. Let's see if the wife arranged this. "Of course, why wouldn't it be?"

"You said he was volatile."

"Not to me!"

"Where were you last night? And your son?"

"Joe was out with his mates, and I was with Belinda and Roger at number one."

"How does Joe get along with his father?"

"Very well. You don't think my son did this, do you? He's only a kid."

"What time did he arrive home?"

"I don't know, I was at Belinda's until half eleven, but he was in bed when I got in, I always check. Will you need to speak to him?"

"Yes, but it can wait until he's back from school. After we've had our tea, while you get ready, I'll nip and see Belinda. We'll take you to the hospital."

"It's okay, I can drive myself."

"You've had a shock. It's best you don't."

While that sounded caring on the surface, the boy in blue helping out a member of the public he served, she suspected he'd want to take note of her face when she saw Pete. Her reaction would be genuine—she never had liked seeing bruises and whatever that came from someone taking a pasting, always gasping at it on the telly.

And in the mirror after he's bashed me.

"Thank you. Oh, I'll need to ring work. Tell my boss I won't be in." She picked her phone up off the table and dialled Lil, gearing herself up for her role.

Sophie brought the tea over and sat beside Mike.

Lil answered after two rings.

"It's me, Amy. I'm so sorry, but I can't come in today. Pete's been beaten up, he was found in an alley this morning, unconscious. He's been taken to hospital. A couple of officers are here, and they're going to drop me down there." Amy pressed the phone

harder against her ear in case Lil's response wasn't fit for police consumption.

"Unconscious? But he was fucking dead when they left him!"

"Poor man, he didn't deserve this." He deserved so much more. "Were you in the pub last night? Did you see him?"

"Is this for the coppers' benefit?"

"Hmm."

"No, I wasn't there. It was best I stayed out of the way, so I went so see Mum in the care home. I can't believe this. What a monumental fuck-up. You'd better go else it'll look suss."

"Thanks. I'll let you know whether I can come in tomorrow."

"Take all the time you need."

Amy wanted to laugh at that, but she held it in, thank goodness. "Bye-bye." *She prodded the* END CALL *icon and put her phone down. Picked up her drink, hands shaking, tea sloshing over the rim.*

"Take a moment to process it all," *Sophie said.*

Amy nodded. Sipped. Thought about what Lil had said. How could Pete have been dead yet he was alive this morning? He must have stopped breathing then started again. Just her fucking luck that even thugs couldn't bump him off. Whoever Amy's guardian angel was, she was doing a pretty shit job of keeping her safe.

She'd drunk half the cup by the time she felt steady enough to speak again. "My boss wasn't in the pub last night, so she can't help."

"Where do you work?" Mike asked.

"Lil's Laundrette."

"What about Pete?"

"He's with Cordite Construction. A brickie. I should phone them, let them know what's happened."

"Don't worry, Sophie can do that."

Sophie took her cup and exited the room, closing the door behind her.

"Are you okay?" Mike asked.

"Not really. Who would be in this situation?"

"Sorry. Stupid question." Mike smiled. Stood. "I'll pop to Belinda's now, then come back for you. Number one, you said?"

"Yes."

He left, leaving Amy to sift through her responses, working out whether she'd said anything that could point the finger at her. She didn't think so, but she fretted just the same. She took the two cups and washed them up, dried them, put them away, then realised she didn't have to leave the house sparkling because Pete was in hospital and wouldn't know. But if she had to spend all day there, playing the dutiful wife, Joe would see any mess after school and report it to his father when he woke up. Pete would store up any infractions and make her pay for them once he was better.

She hoped he died from complications. A severe bleed on the brain. A cracked rib poking into his lung, making it hard to breathe, so much so he suffocated before they could whip him into theatre. Or maybe he'd have a heart attack from the shock of it all, and those paddles they put on your chest couldn't bring him back.

She could hope, couldn't she? She was good at that.

It was all she'd ever done in this train wreck of a marriage.

The men had done a serious number on Pete. Amy supposed thugs for hire weren't in the habit of going lightly on their targets. Had they done it for free, for Lil? Or did they want paying? Would they offer a discount because the job hadn't fucking well been done properly? Because unless Pete died, Amy wouldn't have a penny to give them.

When she'd arrived at the hospital, Pete had been in surgery, so she'd sat for four hours in the family room,

Mike beside her, as though he guarded her, thinking her a criminal. Wasn't that a waste of resources? Wasn't he better off elsewhere, fighting some other crime?

He'd finally left once he'd learned that Pete had been placed in a coma. They'd drained fluid from around his brain, and he needed time to heal. She sat beside the bed in a side room where her bastard of a husband was hooked up to monitors that bleeped. Those bleeps taunted her: He's alive, he's alive, he's alive... She cried, sinking into a pit of moroseness that threatened to drag her under into full-on depression.

No, she wouldn't allow that. She'd come this far, and she could survive for a bit longer. She'd learned to control her emotions, to look cowed on the outside but strong on the inside, and this shit was no different. She'd play the upset wife, while behind the scenes she'd contemplate wrenching those fucking wires and tubes off him and letting the machine do one long, final bleep: He's dead, he's dead, he's deaaaaaaaad... Blocking the door so nurses couldn't come in and revive him. Going to prison for murder—gladly, because she'd really had enough—claiming she cared about him so much that she didn't want Pete to become a vegetable (un-PC, but what did she fucking care right now?). She'd say he'd have wanted her to pull the plug, that they'd discussed this on the many loving nights they'd lain awake talking.

She sent Joe a text, telling him to phone her as soon as he got the chance as something had happened. He'd probably ignore her, thinking she was being neurotic over the recent graffiti in his bedroom, but that was his problem.

What was the point in sitting here? With Pete in a coma, there was nothing she could do, and she was fucked if she was going to talk to him like the doctor had suggested. Encourage him to get better. She got up and walked to the door, the handle cold on her palm, and turned to look at the monster in the bed.

"I hope you die while I'm gone."

Then she left, letting the nurse know she had to get home and break the news to her son and she'd be back in the morning.

"If there's any change, will you let me know?"

"Of course, love."

Amy had to board three busses to get to town, and she entered the Red Lion, needing to know whether Pete's intended end had begun here, seeing as Lil hadn't told her any details. She approached the bar in her jittery, abused persona, Dave spotting her and coming over.

"All right, Amy?"

"I… Did anything happen in here last night?"

"Ah, the police have already been. They told me about Pete. Nasty business. How are you holding up?"

"I've just been to the hospital. His face is all bruised and puffy, and his top lip is swollen and split. He lost a front tooth, has a broken nose, cracked ribs, back and front, and had fluid on the brain so had to have an op. They've put him in a coma."

"Fuck me, love, I'm sorry to hear that. And to answer your question, I'll tell you what I told the Old Bill. Pete got lairy with a couple of toffs. You know how he gets. Took umbrage to them being in here, said they didn't belong. They left, and he went after them. Now, don't get me wrong, they were built, but they didn't strike me as the type to do that to him. Too refined to get their hands dirty, know what I mean? It had to be someone else."

Lil wouldn't know any refined people, so maybe it wasn't the toffs.

"Okay, thanks."

She left, walking to the laundrette. It wouldn't look weird if the police found out she'd come here. Lil was her friend, and Amy needed to chat. She'd have to hurry, though, because someone else would be in for the evening shift in a couple of hours, and Amy didn't want them overhearing anything.

She pushed the door open, the scent immediately putting her at ease, her poor abused psyche recognising it for what it was—the place where she felt safe. Lil folded washing over by one of the machines, and with no customers in, Amy went over and dropped onto a chair.

"You look done in," Lil said.

"I've not long got back from sitting with him. He's in a coma."

Lil folded the last T-shirt then sat, dragging the laundry bag towards her and zipping it up. She took a name tag from her pocket and attached it to the handle. It was Mrs Tolworth's washing, the old cow who always swore at them. Lil had threatened to ban her last time.

"They said he was dead, and I believe them," Lil whispered on a sigh.

Amy checked the door, paranoia setting in. "Who were they? Dave said Pete rowed with a couple of toffs."

Lil laughed. "They do that, pretend to be someone else. I expect they had disguises on an' all."

"Was it The Brothers?"

"No, that would be too obvious if I went to them. I used two heavies from another Estate. I've let them know they failed, so they've said no payment."

"Thank God for that, because I'll get sod all life insurance now unless he snuffs it in hospital. Knowing my luck, he won't. They must have really laid into him, because he's a mess. Had fluid on the brain and everything."

"That'll be the breeze blocks in their briefcases. They whack people round the head with them."

Who the hell thought of such a thing? *"What?"*

"It's their signature weapon. Bloody shame it didn't work. They checked for a pulse, and there wasn't one."

Tears bulged. *"Christ, Lil. I was so hoping to start my new life today."*

"You still could. This is the ideal opportunity to fuck off while he can't stop you."

"But the police might think I'm running away because I'm guilty, thinking I set it up. And I'd have to take Joe. He'd let him know where we've gone."

"How has he taken the news?"

"He doesn't know yet. Hasn't answered my message."

"Bloody kid. So glad I didn't have any." *Lil glanced at the clock.* *"He'll be home from school by now. It's half four."*

"Hmm. I'd better go."

They stood, and Lil drew Amy in for a hug.

"We'll try again, all right?" Lil said. "We'll regroup. Are you working tomorrow?"

"I said I'd nip to the hospital in the morning, but I'll come after. I'll tell the nurses I can't afford to lose my job, what with Pete not getting wages at the minute. That'll stop any speculation."

"Right. We'll talk more then. In the meantime, enjoy the peace without him."

Amy left, thinking there wouldn't be any peace because she still had Joe to contend with. In the crescent, she rushed past Belinda's so she didn't get collared for a gossip—she had no energy for that. She approached her front door with dread soaking into her bones, sending them heavy. She let herself in, only to be confronted immediately by Joe who stood waiting in the hallway, scowling.

"Where's the fucking dinner?"

She struggled to remain calm, but her anger and the unfairness of Pete still being alive poked at her. Earlier, she'd told herself to remain the same, act subservient, but she wasn't sure she'd be able to manage it. "I haven't cooked any yet."

"Why not? You finish work at four, and it's past that now. Where have you been?"

"Sitting in the hospital beside your dad's bed, you arrogant, selfish little bastard. You'd know that if you

read my message and rang me, but no, you didn't want to." She hadn't meant to say that, Joe would tell Pete when he eventually woke up, but she was so angry she didn't give a shit.

Joe slapped her round the face. *"Don't talk to me like that, you cheeky bitch!"*

She stared at him, heat rushing to her skin. *"If you slap me again, I swear to God I'll get hold of the social and tell them everything you've ever done to me. You and your dad. Now get out of my fucking way."*

He wouldn't move, so she brushed him aside and continued into the kitchen. The shove from behind sent her sprawling forward to land on her knees on the kitchen lino, pain spearing up her thighs. It took a moment for her to process what he'd done—why was she even surprised he'd pushed her?—then he gripped the back of her coat and dragged her to standing.

From behind, he whispered in her ear, *"Don't threaten me, you old cow. We both know you'd never see it through."* He released her.

She spun round to face him. *"Don't test me. I've have a bellyful of this life, the shit you two put me through."*

"Look at you, growing a set because Dad isn't here. You wait until he comes home, you'll soon change

then. What's he in hospital for anyway? Accident at work?"

"No, someone beat the shit out of him last night on the way home from the pub. Left him for dead. He's in a coma."

Joe's face drained of colour. "Oh."

"Yes, oh, and the police want to speak to you, see where you were last night."

"What?"

"You heard me. Now make your own dinner for once. I'm going out."

Liberated yet scared to death by her outburst — she'd pay for it in the future — she flounced out, walking to the chippy and buying fish and chips, wishing she'd bought cod for Joe and there was a big bone in it that he'd choke on. She sat on a bench to eat it, her mind full of what-ifs and 'I wish', telling herself she'd be free one day.

Just not today.

Chapter Thirteen

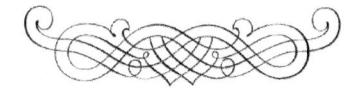

Instead of bagging up the drugs during the night, Joe had got off his face on cocaine, put music on his phone, and danced away his anger over Hailey locking him out and Flint pissing him right off. It had felt good to kick back, to forget for a bit, but it had all come crashing back as soon as he'd opened his bleary eyes this morning.

A strong coffee down his neck, and he was good enough to go, if a bit groggy still. Off to The Angel to hand cash over to Flint, then the trap house to sort the gear for tonight. To pay Flint, he'd had to filch some cash from the takings he'd yet to take to Galaxy's lock-up, but he'd nip to see Hailey later, force her to let him in. Maybe threaten to kill Delaney one day while he was at the play centre with her mum to ensure she opened the door. He'd get some money from the suitcase in her loft and leave her be. No slapping, nothing. That'd mess with her head because she'd be expecting a clout.

He shrugged on his jacket, checked his pocket for his phones, keys, and money envelope, then left his flat, dragging his tired arse down Chancer's Lane. It was fucking cold, so he zipped his coat up and shoved his hands in his pockets. He was late by over an hour but didn't give much of a shit. If Flint wanted his money, he'd wait.

On the way, he accessed the many messages on his line burner. A list as long as his arm wanted drugs, so he forwarded the requests to his runners then stuffed the mobile back in his pocket. Anyone else who messaged in the meantime would have to wait until he'd dropped the cash to Flint.

He sauntered into The Angel, spotting the copper straight away. He had the mad urge to walk right up to him, hand the money over in plain sight, then strut out. That'd teach him. But he couldn't. Flint's threat to take him down was real.

I fucking hate being scared about what he could do to me.

Joe approached the bar and ordered a Coke. He got his wallet out, letting the envelope fall from his pocket onto the floor. He tapped his card on the reader, smiling at the bint behind the bar. There weren't many people in here, just the breakfast crowd, and he glanced round to check if anyone had spotted the envelope, waiting for their chance to pick it up. Everyone was engrossed in either eating a full English, bacon doorsteps, or drinking coffee while scrolling on their phones. Flint, though, he'd seen it from his perch on the dais beneath a super-big clock, his eyes alight, the greedy bastard.

Joe went over to the fruit machine and put in a fiver, his back to Flint. He didn't care one way or the other whether the pig managed to scoop up the money before someone else got their mitts on it—Joe had delivered, Flint had seen that, so his part in the transaction was over. He gulped Coke, stabbing at the buttons on the machine, chuffed with himself for winning twenty quid after a few spins. Pound coins shot out into the tray, and he jabbed the button again for his last go. As luck was on his side today, he might well go to Jackpot Palace for an afternoon of gambling if he got the drugs bagged up quickly enough.

"I'll take a coffee, thank ye."

Joe stiffened at the Irish accent. Was that the bloke from last night? Was Joe being *followed*? He casually peered over his shoulder, but the man at the bar didn't resemble anyone he knew. Different colour hair and beard, and he had a suit on, not those manky baggy clothes.

The woman who'd served Joe—Lisa, her nametag said—leaned across as the Irishman said something to her quietly. She jerked her head in Joe's direction, but the bloke didn't look his way, so maybe she hadn't been indicating him. Still, it bugged Joe, and he'd do well to get out of here.

He pocketed his winnings and left the pub, walking faster than he had on the way here, intent on distancing himself from Flint and that fella. He changed his mind about the order of play, just in case Galaxy messaged to ask why the takings weren't deposited yet. He'd nip to Hailey's now, take enough money out of the loft to replace what he'd borrowed, then go to work. He took the burner out and got on with fielding messages.

The money didn't earn itself, did it.

Chapter Fourteen

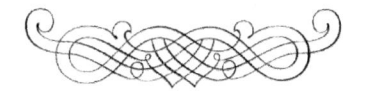

Flint dropped his wallet on top of the envelope and bent to pick both up. Stuffing them in his pocket, he followed Joe out of the pub, keeping back a bit in case he turned round. Mind you, what did it matter if the pleb caught him? He didn't have to explain himself to anyone.

Except the twins.

He grimaced at that.

Last night when he'd got home, he'd logged on to London Teens via a Virtual Private Network, settling in to snag a new target, despite telling himself he should steer clear. His compulsion wouldn't allow it; those young girls were an addiction. He had two laptops, one for pleasure, which he refused to feel guilty about, and one for everything else. That way, if he had to dispose of evidence that would prove what he got up to, he could just dump it, not worrying about losing his innocent links and files.

He'd gone by the name of YOLO, eventually homing in on Gurl_Luvs_Fash. Thirteen, blonde, blue eyes. She looked about eleven, though, and that would mean the cash would come rolling in if he could persuade her to send him pictures of her naked. He'd chatted to her for a while, saying he liked fashion, too, hoping to God that was what 'fash' meant. Thankfully, it did, and he'd said he wanted to be a designer, GOING TO PARIS AND SHIT and RAKING IN THE CASH, INNIT? In between typing to her—she must have been talking to someone else as well, which had bugged him—he'd Googled Fashion Week, amongst other things, so he knew what to talk about.

This bit, the grooming, gave him a thrill like no other. After two hours of chatting about boring things like school and parties, he'd said he had to go to bed.

YOLO: My mum's moaning about me still being up. FML.

Gurl_Luvs_Fash: Yeah, my mum's the same.

YOLO: There's no school tomorrow, so I don't know what the problem is.

Gurl_Luvs_Fash: Mine bangs on about sleep being good for my mental health.

YOLO: Fucking hell, don't!

Gurl_Luvs_Fash: [smiling emoji] You'd better go.

YOLO: Are you on tomorrow night?

Gurl_Luvs_Fash: Yep. [kissy face emoji]

It would take a month or so to get her to really trust him, to believe they were boyfriend and girlfriend, and he'd make sure to ask for the first photo without any makeup on. Then he'd tell her she looked nicer bare-faced, and the best pictures, which she'd send later, would give the impression of a much younger child. His customers were going to love seeing her in the nude.

Flint switched his mind back to the present. If he wasn't careful, he'd be so zoned out he'd lose sight of Joe. He'd gone right at the end of the street, past the women on Debbie's Corner, so Flint meandered the same route he'd taken with that drunk bird last night. Joe didn't turn around, too intent on nosing at his phone, head down. Flint kept his steps light, although they still sounded too loud to him. But Joe didn't go into Chancer's Lane. Instead, he kept going, and the penny dropped.

He's off to Hailey's.

Except he didn't walk down Princeton Avenue but behind it down an alley in Loom Road. Flint stopped close to a brick wall and peered round it. He couldn't risk going down there, Joe was bound to see him when he turned to face the gate, *if* he planned on going into Hailey's via the back door. That *had* to be why he was here, unless he kept going, coming out closer to Kitchen Street.

As predicted, Joe entered her back garden. Flint waited for the gate to shut then crept down the alley. He nosed through a knothole in the fence at eye level. Joe used some kind of tool in the lock, then he was inside.

"Hailey?" Joe called.

With no response, he shut the door.

Flint went into the garden, quickly in case Joe went upstairs and looked out, spotting him. The curtains were open up there, but the blinds were down on the back door and the window beside it. Taking a chance that Joe wouldn't be on the other side, Flint opened the door.

Thudding footsteps—he must be going upstairs.

Flint closed the door and waited for a few seconds. At the sound of a *donk*, then the unmistakable screech of a ladder coming down, he was likely going into the loft. Why? Did he store drugs up there without Hailey's knowledge? No, there was a lock-up for that. It must be where he kept his money.

Flint recalled the other night when he'd told Hailey everything in the Red Lion. He'd been drunk and wanted to get back at Joe in any way he could, any way it would hurt, so he'd enjoyed blabbing. He'd warned her to stay away from Joe if she knew what was good for her, saying she'd get nicked along with him—the police would assume she was in the county line somehow, and if she valued her freedom, she ought to listen to what he'd said.

The poor cow was visibly hurt that Joe had lied to her, and she'd seemed confused, too, as though she couldn't understand how the man she cared for was someone so completely different to what he'd shown her.

"The Brothers will sort him for you," he'd said. "Just ask and you will receive."

He'd laughed at his own joke, but she hadn't.

"This isn't funny, you know. This is my life you're taking the piss out of."

"Sorry, sorry."

More footsteps, tinny this time. Joe was going up the ladder. A metal one?

Flint inched along the hallway, then up the stairs. The loft hatch yawned above him, a rectangular gaping mouth, the roof crisscrossed with splinter-riddled rafters, light from a dusty bulb illuminating the wooden beams. Flint nipped into the bathroom at the other end of the landing, opposite, so he could see when Joe came down with whatever he'd gone up there for. What if he brought money down? If Flint played his cards right, he could nick it off him. The kid must have earned thousands by now.

Flint spied through the gap by the hinges.

And waited.

Chapter Fifteen

Ichabod had messaged the twins to let them know Joe had been in The Angel and what had occurred—he'd come in just as the little eejit had dropped an envelope.

GG: Keep an eye on him. We're not ready to apprehend him yet. We've got someone else to speak to first. If he leaves, tail him.

Ichabod had ordered coffee but hadn't had a chance to drink it. Joe had sidled out, and a man had picked up the envelope, Ichabod quickly snapping a picture of him discreetly. The man had then walked out. Why the fuck had he followed Joe? Did the envelope contain instructions or something?

Ichabod had sent the picture to the twins.

GG: Fuck me, that's Flint! What the hell's going on?

The shock of that had momentarily stalled Ichabod, and he'd replied: Tailing them now.

All the way to Hailey's back gate, neither man had turned to check behind them. Ichabod always employed stealth, but come on, you'd think they'd be a bit more careful. Their lack of common sense astounded him. Joe had been on his phone, and Flint must have been so intent on going after him that he'd only concentrated on that. *Why* was the copper after Joe, though? Was Joe on the police radar for the drugs?

After Ichabod had left the parlour to get hold of Mason, going to Joe's street and waiting there, Greg had messaged him an update as to what Joe had been getting up to and how Hailey and Joe's ex, Stacey, had suffered. Maybe Flint worked for the NCA, the drugs department. The twins hadn't told him much about the man, so it was possible he'd already had Joe in his sights before he'd started working for them.

Both men had gone into Hailey's garden, so Ichabod had pursued. In the house, he'd prowled the lower floor, finding no one. Then he'd gone upstairs and, finding the loft hatch open, had dipped into a bedroom. Hailey's lad's.

Now, door left open the same amount as it had been before he'd gone in there (he didn't want to arouse suspicion), he pressed himself to the wall and eyed the loft hatch, taking out his phone.

ICHABOD: IN H'S HOUSE. CAN'T SEE J OR F, BUT THE LOFT IS OPEN.

He waited for the mobile to vibrate against his hand.

GG: WTF? H SAYS THERE'S NOTHING UP THERE. SHE STORES HER STUFF IN THE SHED. IF YOU GET THE CHANCE, APPREHEND J. WING IT WITH F, BUT I WANT HIM WITH YOU WHEN YOU BRING J IN. THIS CAN BE HIS INITIATION.

ICHABOD: WAIT. MOVEMENT.

He slid his phone away, taking his gun out. If Flint didn't belong to the twins, Ichabod would have kept it hidden, but the man would have to turn a blind eye if he saw it. The rules were different now, lines blurred, and Flint would have to get used to it. Ichabod outranked him.

He smiled at that.

Joe came down the ladder backwards, one of his tracksuit bottom pockets bulging. It didn't look like he was packing, the bulge wasn't the right shape for a shooter, but still, Ichabod would remain wary.

He aimed his gun, ready.

Joe shoved the ladder up then jumped to push the hatch shut. It wouldn't catch, so he tried again, successful this time. He turned, spotted Ichabod, and froze.

"Don't bother runnin'. Sit, nice and slow."

Joe glanced to the top of the stairs.

"I'll shoot ye before ye even take one step, ye feckin' moron. Bullets are faster than ye are. *Sit.*"

Joe lowered to his haunches, likely ready to spring away.

"On ye arse!"

A sigh, and Joe plonked himself down. "Who the fuck *are* you?"

"I can be ye worst nightmare, but there are two others more worthy of that title than me. One more than the other."

"What are you on about?"

"The twins. I told ye last night Hailey was under their protection, yet here ye are, in her house, thievin' somethin' from her loft."

"I fucking *knew* it was you in the pub just now."

"My accent gave me away, did it?"

"Fuck you and your sarcasm."

Ichabod smiled. "Flint, I know ye're in here. Ye can come out now."

"*Flint*?" Joe's eyes narrowed, and he darted them left to right, then they widened, focused ahead. "What the hell are *you* doing here?"

Ichabod stepped onto the landing, his gun still trained on Joe. Flint appeared in his peripheral.

"I'd like tae know the same thing, as would The Brothers." Ichabod would love to turn and see Flint's face, read it for signs of deception, but he didn't trust this Joe bastard not to get up and run.

Flint cleared his throat, then his breathing lengthened. "Joseph Osbourne, you are under arrest for intent to supply. You have the right to remain silent. You do not have to say anything, but—"

"Ah, shut ye feckin' trap," Ichabod said. "He doesn't deserve tae be under arrest for what he's done. There's another punishment waitin' for him."

"You absolute bellend," Joe said to Flint, rising slowly to his feet, his hands raised, palms out. "I gave you that money, I held up my side of the bargain. What the fuck, man?"

"You were part of an undercover surveillance operation," Flint said. "Except I wasn't exactly undercover because you know I'm a police officer, but you fell for it, for everything I said. What a fucking clown. What did you come here for? Not that I can't guess. This is where you store your cash, isn't it? Which is why I followed you in here. If I can seize money earned via illegal gains, and your prints are all over it, you're fucked."

"The runners. What about them?" Joe asked. "Or was that more bullshit, that they were going to be rounded up in a few days?"

"It's today." Flint sounded smug.

"You fucking bastard!"

Ichabod would have to butt in. Now wasn't the time for these two to hash it out. "I know who ye are, Flint, and what ye're expected tae do, so there won't be any arrest today, and no one's takin' money out of that loft. I'm safe tae say that the twins will be on the same page as me—that money is in Hailey's house, therefore, it belongs tae her now. Payment for all the shite this feckin' wanker's put her through. Maybe she'll split it wid Stacey."

Joe paled. "What?"

"Ye heard me. We know everythin'." Ichabod took a cable tie out of his pocket and held it out. "Tie his wrists behind his back, Mr Policeman." Then to Joe, "Turn around and face the wall, ye scrote."

Joe darted towards the stairs. Ichabod fired a shot into his foot, the silencer dulling the noise a little. Joe hopped around, screeching. Flint brushed past Ichabod and wrestled Joe down onto his front, pressing his knee into his back and wrenching both arms up at an alarming angle.

"You're fucking *hurting* me!" Joe snarled.

"That's the plan." Flint attached the cable tie expertly then hauled the prick to his feet. He turned to Ichabod. "I take it the twins are onto him which is why you're here?"

"Give yeself a gold star. Now, we're going on a little trip." He took his phone out and messaged Martin who should be parked out the front.

ICHABOD: GO TO THE END OF THE STREET AND TAKE A LEFT DOWN LOOM ROAD. PARTWAY ALONG, THERE'S AN ALLEY THAT GOES BEHIND HAILEY'S. STOP THERE AND WAIT.

MARTIN: ON IT.

Ichabod smiled at Flint. "Take him downstairs. This will be ye first job for the twins?"

"Yeah."

Joe, his face wet with tears of pain, glanced between the two of them, then focused on the copper. "You work for the *twins*?"

Flint laughed. "Welcome to my world, shit for brains. I told you I was under pressure, and I said I'd have you, didn't I? Well, here we are…"

Chapter Sixteen

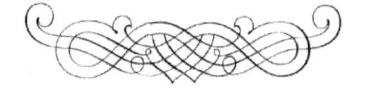

There was something satisfying about being at Pete's beck and call this time, because he was in bed and had to piss in a pot and shit on a commode. The indignity of it would embarrass him. Emasculate him. Good. She left him to go to work, uncaring that he might mess the bed and have to lie in it. In fact, she prayed he would and was always disappointed when

she came back to see the sheets were still clean. She'd have liked to let him fester in it, get bed sores. She'd been sleeping on the sofa, so it wouldn't have affected her.

He'd been out of hospital for two weeks, and during that time, her urge to continue suffering until she could finish him off had taken a firmer hold. Warped, she must be, to put herself through this, but the ultimate aim to have the last say, the last laugh, wouldn't let go. The sensible side of her knew she should leave, but those vines she'd imagined had tightened, squeezing her into compliance, and as she had no desire to start again with another bloke, she may as well stay and see this through.

It was a delicious game, and while she'd get beaten up again once Pete had healed, have abuse hurled at her, she'd endure it if it meant she got what she wanted in the end: the life insurance payout, money she deserved for everything he'd put her through. A nice little earner for all her hard work and misery. She'd travel, see a bit of the world instead of this pocket in the East End. She'd eat out twice a week, buy new shoes before the soles wore thin.

She placed the tray of dinner on his lap—sausage and mash, peas, gravy, a little tub of jelly for afters, and a glass of orange juice. She sat on the chair in the corner to watch him struggle to eat it, because she hadn't cut the sausages up. Moving his arms brought on jabbing pains to his rib cage, and he slept sitting up, several pillows behind him. A laugh bubbled into her throat, and she pushed it down and placed her phone on the small table next to her, facedown so he wouldn't see the RECORD *button on the screen.*

He hadn't said much since he'd come home, until last night; maybe his fat lip had prevented it. She'd wondered whether the beating had taught him the biggest lesson of his life, except he'd proved it hadn't by calling her a fucking slag when she'd 'accidentally' tipped the tray of food on him last night as she'd put it down, boiling-hot curry going all over his bare belly. It had scalded, and he'd roared in pain.

"How was your day?" she asked to rile him up.

"Fucking peachy. How do you think it was, you stupid bitch?" Air whistled through the gap where he'd lost his tooth.

"I was only making conversation."

"What have I told you about not speaking until you're spoken to?"

"You've told me a lot, actually. You've said it every day for years."

"So why hasn't it sunk in yet? Oh, I forgot, you're thick as pig shit."

"Not if the pig's got the runs," she said.

He glared at her. "Think you're funny, do you? You just wait until I'm better. I'll knock seven bells out of you. Joe's told me what you said to him that night. How dare you talk to my boy like that."

"How dare you two pick on me, hit me, abuse me."

"You deserve it. Women should know their place."

She sighed. The same old mantra.

It was all well and good her speaking to him like this while he was stuck in bed, only able to make it to the commode, but like he'd said, when he was better…

But she didn't plan for him to get better.

She glanced at the extra-strong pain pills on the bedside cabinet, ones he'd got from the hospital. Lil had given her the idea. Crush them all up and put them in a cup of tea, watch him drink it. Wash the cup up with bleach to remove all traces of the drug. Wait for him to die, then act shocked that he'd 'killed himself'. She'd say it must have been the torment of being bedbound that had sent him down that path or that his brain had been damaged.

"Where's Joe?" he asked.

"Why, are you going to ask him to hit me because you can't?"

"I mean it, Amy…"

"He's out with that gang again, I expect."

"That kid's going to go far. He's a natural leader."

Pete finally trusted his food enough for it not to be piping hot—he had a bare chest again today, and it pleased her he was worried about being burnt again. He speared a sausage with a fork, saying, "Ouch!" He ate, the sound of him chomping enough for anyone to commit murder, but she hid her disgust, as usual.

"I'm going to find those men and kill them." He loaded up some mash, a couple of peas stuck to it. "Fucking posh tossers."

"What, actually kill them?"

"I wasn't just saying it for the fun of it."

She smiled at that being caught on the recording. "The police haven't had any luck, so I don't know how you'll fare any better. You're not exactly Poirot, are you."

"Are you saying I won't be able to do it?"

She ignored him. He shovelled mash into his mouth, one forkful after another until it was all gone, then attacked the other sausage.

"I'm struggling with you only getting sick pay," she said. "The bills are behind."

"So? You'll cope, you always do."

His lack of care failed to surprise her. "I'm thinking of getting another job in the evenings." So I don't have to see you.

"You do that. Then you can serve me better meals."

"There's nothing wrong with sausage and mash."

"That's reminded me. When I was in hospital, nothing tasted of salt, yet now I'm back home again, and this gravy is full of it."

"Blame the cheaper brand I had to buy. Unless you hand over some of your savings you like to brag about, you'll have to do without your Bisto."

He stared at her. "I don't like your tone."

"I don't like the way you bully me and treat me like shit, but here we are."

It was safe, to do this, to air her thoughts and feelings, because she'd made up her mind. He was going to commit hari-kari tonight, although not in the real sense. He wouldn't be disembowelling himself in a ritual like the Japanese, a lesson she remembered from school because it had shocked and sickened her so much, all that pain. It was called Seppuku, she'd never forget it, and it meant 'cutting the belly'. While she'd love to sink a knife into his, she'd have to be content with the fact she'd scalded it with that curry.

Now she'd definitely decided on her next move, she could stop recording the conversation, but she wouldn't. If the last murder attempt was anything to go by, this one could also go wrong so she'd still need the insurance.

He poked his fork towards her, his expression scrunching, showing how much that movement had hurt. "You'd better watch yourself, woman."

"Or what?"

He shook his head. "Or I'll sort you out."

"That could mean many things, though. What, exactly, would you do?"

"You know that carving knife we've got?"

"Of course. I use it enough, seeing as I'm the only one around here who cooks because you said it's 'my place'."

"I'd stab it right in your heart. Bury you in Daffodil Woods."

"Oh right, and how would you get away with that? The police always suspect the spouse." Her stomach rolled over at that. Would they think she'd given him the drugs?

"Ways and means. Just sleep with one eye open, that's all I'm saying."

"Sounds like a threat to my life."

He sighed. "It is. Weren't you listening?*"*

"I just wanted to make sure."

He eyed her, then dug a spoon in his jelly. "What the fuck are you up to?"

"Nothing apart from running around after you, as usual. What does it feel like to treat me as a skivvy and

a punchbag? To see me walking around with hidden bruises and broken bones because you hurt me? To tell me I'm useless, will never amount to anything, and the only thing I'm good for is lying on my back or standing at the kitchen sink? Or how about that time you said if you could chain me to your wrist and cart me about with you, you would, so I was like a slave."

"Why do you need to know what it feels like? Just put up and shut up." He rammed the jelly in his mouth, wincing again. He must keep forgetting about those ribs. He finished the pot and pushed the tray down his legs, his signal for her to come and get it.

She rose. Popped the phone in her cardigan pocket. Took the tray and moved to open the door. She turned back to look at him. "I don't want to do that anymore, put up and shut up. I don't deserve it, and I'm thinking of reporting you to the police."

She walked out to his shouted protestations, locking the door so he couldn't come after her — it would take him too long to get out of bed anyway, his ribs too sore for him to use any speed. She pocketed the key, switched the recording off, and went downstairs, glad Joe had already eaten and gone out. He was staying over at a mate's tonight as it was a Friday, up to God knew what, so it was the perfect opportunity to do what had to be done.

Doing the washing up, she went through the steps for later. She'd also have to bleach the wooden rolling pin she'd use to crush the tablets, clean the worktop afterwards, burn the cloth she'd wiped with. Or maybe crushing them between two sheets of baking paper, then burning the paper would work better. Who knew if they'd send those forensic people in here. He had a glass of water already on the bedside, half full, so it would look like he'd drunk that to wash the tablets down. Yes, the pathologist would find the tea in his stomach, or maybe in his bladder, but that was okay. She only had to hope that the pills, had he taken them whole, would have dissolved by the time he died, otherwise that would be a massive red flag.

Satisfied she had everything in order, she watched the telly for a bit then popped down to Belinda's. Roger was out, thank goodness, off playing in a darts tournament, so they got to chat in the living room over a pot of tea.

"Pete said he wants to kill himself," Amy lied.

"A blessing in disguise. One less bastard on the planet." Belinda smiled. "It's just a shame he didn't die in that fight. I prayed he would, you know."

"So did I, but luck's never been on my side, has it."

"What's he want to kill himself for?"

"He said his brain doesn't feel right since he got beaten up. Like it's sluggish or something."

"Maybe his attacker damaged it more than the hospital realised. You hear about that happening, don't you. You only need one bad kick to the nut and it can send you do-lally. Has he been acting differently, then? Slurring his words an' all that?"

"Yes. I should let the doctor know really, or maybe phone the hospital."

"Why? He won't be able to top himself, then." Belinda tittered. *"I shouldn't laugh, shouldn't even think this conversation is remotely okay, but my God, the things he's done to you. Let him send himself to Hell. You'll only have another three years with Joe, then you can kick him out. Or if he misbehaves in the meantime, get the social involved. They'll take him away to the kiddie nuthouse, because that's where he belongs. They'll give him therapy; he fucking needs it. That boy's mental. Pete ruined him. Look what a lovely little lad he was until his father put his oar in."*

"I often wonder what he'd have been like if I could have brought him up how I wanted."

"You'll never know, so don't beat yourself up over it. 'Ere, have you come to mine for an alibi? So Pete can get on and do what he needs to do?"

"No, I just had to get away from him for a bit. I barely see him anymore, what with work and everything, but even the hour or so I spend with him is too long. I was so pissed off about it I burnt him with a curry last night, all over his belly."

Belinda roared. "I'd have loved to have seen that."

"It must have really hurt because it's still red now."

They laughed together, Amy sounding a tad unhinged, so she reined it in, focusing on the task ahead to keep her mind balanced—if killing your husband could be classed as such. An hour of slagging Pete off passed, then she left Belinda's, going indoors to the beautiful sound of silence. She put on her rubber gloves and crept upstairs, unlocking the door quietly, finding Pete asleep. She heaved at the smell of shit. He must have used the commode. She collected the two packets of tablets, locked him in again, and returned downstairs. Did what she had to do and added the white dust to a cup of tea, putting in more sugar to override any bitterness. She shoved the cloth and baking paper in the living room fire.

Back in the bedroom, she dropped the empty pill boxes on the bedside table, then moved around the other side of the bed to wake him, breathing through her mouth.

"I've brought you a cuppa." She placed it on her nightstand and stepped out of reach.

He gazed up at her, bleary-eyed, then struggled to sit up better.

She let him, no way was she going to help.

Pete glared at her. "If I could get out of this bed, I'd teach you a lesson for all the crap you spouted earlier."

"You could get out, you do to use the commode, but your ribs are so fucked that if you hit me, you'll hurt yourself more."

"Speaking of the commode, it needs cleaning. Fucking stinks."

"I'm aware. I can smell it. You're a filthy pig."

"You're going to regret speaking to me the way you have."

"I doubt it."

"What the fuck's got into you?"

"It's called deciding not to play this sick game anymore. It's called stop dicking around and change things. It's called telling your husband that you've been biding your time for years, pretending he has control, when in fact, I do."

He laughed, wincing at the pain the movement must have produced. "You're off your tree if you think you can get away with this."

"I must have been to stay here and tolerate you, all for what, to make a point?"

He frowned. "What are you talking about?"

"Forget it. You've always said my thoughts don't matter. Drink your tea."

He eyed her, clearly trying to work things out and coming up empty.

She sat on the chair, taking her phone out to scroll through the news. "On this day in history"—the day you finally snuff it—*"ten people have died in an avalanche, a thirteen-year-old boy has been stabbed and killed in south London"*—shame it wasn't Joe—*"and an MP in the Labour party has resigned."*

"I couldn't give less of a fuck, Amy." He sipped his tea and cringed. *"What the hell is this?"*

"Tea!"

"Tastes like gnat's piss."

"Have you ever drunk that?"

"Of course I sodding well haven't."

"Then how do you know what it tastes like?"

"You're seriously grinding my gears, woman. Any more of your lip, and I'll ring Joe. He'll give you a pasting." He sipped some more. *"This has got to be one those newfangled teas, because it's not right."*

"I can't afford PG Tips anymore. I've already told you I'm struggling." Not for much longer once I

get that life insurance, arsehole. *She'd already checked, and it paid out for suicide, so long as it occurred four years after taking the policy out.*

"*I don't like it when you're like this. Remember what happened when you changed before? When you ran to Belinda's and Roger ratted you out?*"

"*Yes, you broke my wrist.*"

"*This time, I'll break your fucking neck.*"

She could tell by his eyes he meant it, that in this moment, if he could, he'd put his hands around her throat and squeeze.

She smiled. "*Good luck getting away with that.*"

His eyebrows crawled together to meet in the middle. "*What do you mean by that?*"

"*I recorded our conversation earlier, the one where you said you'd kill me. I went to Belinda's and played it to her, then I sent it to her so she's got a copy.*" *Lies, lies, and more lies.* "*And if you're thinking of getting Roger to go on her phone and delete it, she's emailed it to a secret account she's got.*"

To her shock, he didn't answer, just sipped thoughtfully, staring at her the whole time. It should unnerve her, but it didn't, because by the time he lumbered out of that pit, she'd be long gone, and he'd be locked in again.

"Why have you been sleeping downstairs?" he asked out of the blue. "Just because I'm poorly, doesn't mean you can get away with not having sex. You can suck me off and not hurt me."

His change of subject didn't faze her, he often did that to throw her off.

"I might hurt you, though. You know, bite your cock off."

This game of chess would be so dangerous in other circumstances, but while she had the chance to stand up for herself, to talk to him like shit, she would.

"You what?"

She laughed. "I can see the appeal in bullying someone now. It feels pretty good, so I get why you and Joe do it."

He drained the rest of his tea and flung the cup at her. It missed her, smacking into the wall and smashing into three pieces. She stood, bent to pick them up, and walked to the door.

"For that, I'm going to lock you in, leave you to breathe in the stench coming out of the commode all night."

She left, laughing as she turned the key in the lock.

Revenge was sweet.

Even sweeter in the morning when she went in there and found him dead.

Chapter Seventeen

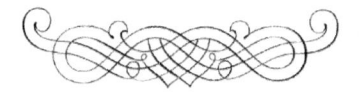

Stacey couldn't stop shaking. Sitting beside Hailey, the twins on the sofa in front of them, had been scary at first, until Hailey had whispered that Greg was nice, George not so much (he had a bit of a bark on him), but he'd turned out all right, and Hailey had ended up liking him, even if he did scare her silly. Stacey had soon found out what 'a bit of a bark' meant. George had so far alternated between being calm and collected then switching to a raving monster, swearing and listing all the things he wanted to do to Joe.

"I'll cut off his cock."

"I'll make him choke on his bollocks."

"I'll ram my cricket stump in his ears."

"I'll string him up on the rack and whip him with razor wire like Cassie."

Who Cassie was, she had no idea, but she sounded a right nasty bitch if that's what she did to inflict pain on people. George had soon explained.

"There's this bird, she was a leader of sorts up north. Lovely woman, if a bit nutty when the occasion called for it. A bit like me: nice until you pissed her off. She had this meat mincer, used to feed dead bodies into it—bloody genius idea. Our version of chopping them up and dropping the pieces in the Thames. That's what's going to happen to Joe, by the way. He'll just seem to disappear."

Stacey had blinked at the visual, seeing human mince coming out of a giant pipe, and she'd wanted to throw up.

Forcing herself to go back into the past had been difficult. She'd glossed over everything during her chats with Hailey, no need to go into any depth because Hailey had suffered the same herself so knew the score. But George insisted on probing, wanting a list of every infraction. She'd just recounted the first rape, glossing as much as possible again. They didn't need to know every rancid detail of it, and she had no energy to say anything else on the subject.

But it looked like she was going to have to.

George leaned forward and draped his hands between his open knees. "I get that this is hard, I really do, and you're emotionally tired, I can see that, but if you want us to lay charges at Joseph's door, to have him answer what I put to him, to apologise for every crime, then I need to know everything. I don't want a blow-by-blow account, just what he did. You said he violated you. Did he cut you before that or after?" He indicated her wrist tattoo.

"After the second rape."

"You what?"

She sighed. "He did it five times altogether."

Hailey stared at her. "You didn't tell me that! You said your brothers went and beat him up after he cut you."

"They did. I just didn't specify *which* cut. That's why I had a new quilt, because I'd bought one after every fucking episode." Stacey shouldn't snap at her, but George was right, she was tired.

He got up and paced. "I'm going to hurt that motherfucker so badly he won't be able to see straight. Did you stay with him out of fear?"

Was he stupid? "Of course I did!"

"What prompted you to finally tell your brothers?" Greg asked, giving his twin a filthy look that seemed to say: *Really? You even had to ask her that?*

"Because he cut me down there. Took a knife to it." Saying that out loud was as liberating as it was awful.

George punched the wall, muttering, "Fuck off. Not yet. Just fuck off, all right? Calm it down, it won't be long, then you can take over."

Stacey glanced at Hailey.

"His Hulk's bothering him," Hailey said.

Stacey shook her head. His Hulk? This was confusing, and she wanted to run. Go home and wait for Chaz to come home, forget everything again. But Chaz was away for work and wouldn't be back until Tuesday.

"I… This is all way too much." Stacey took a deep breath. "Okay, fine, he cut me, and my brothers gave him a kicking. Joe didn't bother me again, the end." She wasn't going to put herself through explaining the intricacies, there was no need.

"Did you go to hospital?" George sat, two of his knuckles bleeding.

"Yes, he sliced part of my labia off inside."

Hailey shrieked, and George closed his eyes.

"I am so fucking sorry you went through that," he said. "What the hell did you tell the nurse?"

"Said I'd done it while shaving. That the razor slipped."

"Why didn't you come to us? We'd have killed him on the spot."

"Ever heard of shame?" Stacey asked, for some reason wanting to hurt him. He was trying his best to understand, but he never would, so maybe she ought to give him an insight. "Shame and feeling stupid for staying with him for so long. Embarrassed because I was twenty-three going out with an eighteen-year-old. A cradle snatcher, some people called me, but I thought I loved him." She laughed. "Now I've gone to the other extreme and shacked up with an older man. Charles Landgraf, if you need to know—but I do *not* want him being told about this. I healed down there, so he's none the wiser."

"Why have you never told him?" George asked. "The shame?"

"No, by that point, I wasn't ashamed, I'd been to therapy, I knew what Joe did wasn't my fault. I didn't want to relive it, that's why."

"And I've just made you go through that." George sighed. "I'm sorry."

"You've probably done me a favour. I've faced it all again and I'm still standing. The world didn't fall down around me."

"We know how that goes," Greg said. "It's safer to tuck the past away, but once you get it out in the open, you feel better, even if it was a painful process. Sometimes, the fear of opening up is more scary than the actual act of spewing it out."

Stacey felt for him. "You sound like you have firsthand experience."

"We do. But this isn't about us. Do you think you'll need more therapy after this chat? We can arrange that for you. It's free."

"So I heard. But no, thank you. I'll be all right so long as he ends up dead."

"Can you handle knowing we killed him for you?" George came over and crouched before her. Took her hands in his. "It's harder than you think, knowing you gave the nod. Some people cope with it fine, they even help us kill, but others, they can't get over it. You've been through a lot, and I don't want to add to it."

"Are you *kidding* me? After what you just made me tell you?"

"I explained why we needed to know."

"But you could have had more tact." Gone were the days when Stacey didn't stick up for herself. George needed to know he'd crossed a line.

Greg ran hand through his hair. "I tell him that all the time, love. Just know he means well, and if he's been told all the details, it fires him up. Or the Hulk anyway." He smiled.

"Right, but go about it more gently in future, will you? Some people won't have developed a thick skin like me."

George nodded. "Honestly, I'm sorry. I just…I fucking *hate* people like him."

"Join the club. I want to slice his throat. Tell me where and when, and I'll do it." Stacey meant it, too. The only way she could exorcise these demons was to eradicate the devil himself, to know he wasn't in a position to do this to anyone else. She already felt bad enough that he'd gone on to hurt Hailey. "I hate him more than you'll ever know." She clutched Hailey's hand. "What about you? Are you with me?"

"I'll be there."

Tears burned Stacey's eyes. "We'll do it together, like we said."

Hailey nodded and looked at George. "Shall I bring the knife I bought?"

He let go of Stacey's hands and stood. "Fuck no, I've got plenty of weapons you can use."

A phone went off beside Greg who picked it up and held it out.

George took it and read the screen. Smiled. "The target has been apprehended. Seems he *has* been stashing his money in your loft, Hailey."

Hailey shook her head. "Bastard."

"You might well be a very rich woman, although Ichabod said it would be nice to share it with Stacey."

"But I don't *want* drug money," Hailey said.

Stacey squeezed her hand. "It's that compensation I mentioned. And think about what you could do with it. We can't spend it willy-nilly, it'd look suss, but it'll bloody well help over the years. If you don't want it, I'll take the lot. He *owes* me."

George looked at Stacey. "Yeah, you're ready. I can see it in your eyes."

She rose to her feet. "Yep, especially because it means I'll be home in time for dinner."

George laughed. "That depends on how long I torture him."

She shivered. This was it. They were doing it.

It was *her* time to get blood on her hands and money in her pocket.

Fuck you, Joe.

Chapter Eighteen

Flint stood in front of a metal contraption on the wall, lethal spikes sticking out of the frame. It must be used for torture, and he dreaded to think what it would feel like to have those nasty tips digging into his skin. Manacles hung at each corner, giving him the willies.

He'd lied at Hailey's house about why he'd gone there, but what else could he have done with the Irishman turning up? He'd have gone and tattled to the twins in a heartbeat if Flint hadn't made out he'd been undercover, fucking about with Joe, all in the name of the law. He reckoned the Irish bloke had swallowed it, but all the same, he was crapping it now. The twins were on the way, and God knew what they'd say to him.

Flint was annoyed with himself. He'd been so intent on tailing Joe that he hadn't made himself aware of his surroundings. He hadn't noticed someone had followed him. To ensure he didn't fuck up while working for the twins, he'd better up his game. Irish must have been laughing his head off at him.

I should know better. I'm a fucking copper!

"Just so ye know, my name's Ichabod. Obviously, I work for the twins. I'm one of their top men, so tae speak."

Flint nodded. "Right."

"So, this is what happens next." Ichabod stared at Joe. "You're goin' tae take all of your clothes off."

"What?" Joe shrieked, his head whipping between Flint and Ichabod. "You'd better be joking."

Flint chuckled. God, *how* long had he waited for this little prick to be taken down a peg? He'd enjoy his humiliation, the torture, which was sure to come. But why did he need to be naked?

Probably so it's easier to cut him or whatever.

"I'm not undressing for no man," Joe muttered.

Ichabod stepped closer and pressed the dangerous end of his gun to Joe's temple, pushing so hard the skin indented. "Oh, ye will." He swung his head to smile at Flint. "On that table is a selection of tools. Can ye get a knife tae cut this cable tie?"

Flint appreciated being asked instead of told. Gladly, he walked over there, finally getting to see the array of weapons he and his colleagues had often speculated about. There were more than he'd imagined, some of them shit he'd never seen before, like they belonged in the olden days. He selected a normal modern knife and returned to the captive—he liked thinking of him as that—slicing the plastic, poking the tip of the blade into Joe's upper arm, a warning in case he thought of lashing out now his hands were free. It would only take one slip, and the steel would glide right through his clothes and skin, smacking into bone.

"Take your clothes off," Flint said in his ear, hoping his breath was hot enough to either repulse or give Joe chills. "There's a good boy."

Joe shuddered too quick to disguise it. Flint smiled. He'd always liked fucking with people like him, scaring the shit out of them, using control and threats to turn gobby kids into whimpering babies.

Joe gritted his teeth. "Fuck you."

Ichabod's finger tightened on the trigger, then he lowered the gun to poke it into Joe's back on one side. "I can't shoot ye in the head because the twins will want a word wid ye, but I *can* shoot ye in the body. If ye don't do as ye told, a bullet will find its way into ye kidney. Who knows, George and Greg might stop off on the way for somethin' tae eat, so it'll be a long while wid you bleedin' all over the place—*in pain*."

Joe's bottom lip wobbled. "You pair of savage cunts."

Flint laughed. "You haven't seen anything yet. Wait until you meet the twins."

Joe dropped his trackie bottoms, kicking his trainers off, the bottoms following. One white sock had a hole in it, and blood had seeped from the bullet wound he'd acquired at Hailey's. It looked like it had shattered the thin bones. "Can you take that fucking gun and knife away so I can get my top half off? Jesus, give a man some space, will you?"

Flint sighed. "In your position, I wouldn't be dishing out orders. Just shows how much self-importance runs through you. You're one of the most entitled pricks I know. I'm glad it's all coming to an end."

"I'd like you to explain to your DCI where the fuck I am tomorrow."

"Easy. You legged it."

Flint and Ichabod took a step back.

Joe shirked his jacket off, then pulled his T-shirt over his head, revealing a hard torso, his stomach muscles something to be envied. Flint had never owned a belly like that. While he wasn't flabby, he'd never had it in him to spend time at a gym. Joe's bulging upper arms spoke of hours lifting weights, yet he wasn't a big lad in stature, more wiry than anything.

"Boxers and socks, too, eejit." Ichabod kicked the other clothing away.

"You've got to be joking." Joe stared at him.

"Does this face look like I'm laughin'?"

Joe's face flared red, and he bent to take his socks off then surged forward, ramming his head into Ichabod's groin. Flint automatically raised the knife, harking back to his beat days when he'd wielded a baton, bringing it down into the space to the far side of Joe's shoulder blade. The resultant screech echoed, and Joe stagger-limped away, a hand reaching round for the wound. He headed for the tools on display. Flint dropped the knife and lunged after him, tackling him down. He sat on his back, pressing his face to the floor extra hard for the fuck of it, Joe's nose squashed.

"You are *really* starting to get my goat, kid. This isn't a game where you can fold and leave the card table. Now I'm going to ask nicely, and if you try anything like that again, Ichabod *will* shoot you, understand?"

"You're a fucking bent pig bastard. Get *off* me!"

Flint did that, wrenching Joe to his feet and holding his wrists behind his back. Ichabod tucked the gun in his holster and stepped forward. He yanked Joe's boxers down, laughed, then kneed him in the dick. Joe bent double in pain, blood seeping from his back wound to drip down his side and onto the floor.

"Get him on the feckin' chair."

Flint dragged a growling Joe to the wooden seat, forcing him to sit, standing behind him, one hand on his shoulder, the other placed over his wound on the other side, digging his finger into the exposed flesh. Joe screeched, arms flailing.

"Hold those feckers down for me."

Flint crouched and did as he was told, using all his strength to keep a bucking Joe in place. Ichabod collected a coil of rope and got on with layering it around and around Joe's body and the back of the chair, pinning his arms to his sides.

Flint stood and picked up the knife, then walked to stand in front of Joe. "You really need to learn when to know you're beaten."

"Galaxy's going to kill you for this," Joe spat.

Ichabod frowned. "What the feck has a bar of chocolate got tae do wid anythin'?"

"It's his boss, the supplier to the county line." Flint smirked at Joe. "Isn't that right? Except Galaxy will do nothing because he's being arrested today like everyone else."

That was an outright lie. Galaxy would think Joe had done a runner with his earnings as well as the drugs in the trap house. Flint would have to tell the twins about that. Make out he was on their side. That's why he'd stabbed Joe just now. Mr Irish could tell them Flint was well and truly a Cardigan Estate employee, nothing to worry about here. George had mentioned an initiation, videoing him killing someone for insurance, but Flint reckoned he'd already proved his loyalty. On the outside at least. Inside, he was loyal only to himself.

"Is your knife wound hurting even more because it's clamped against that chair?" Flint asked.

"You know it is," Joe muttered. "What are you, some kind of sadist who gets off on someone in pain?"

No, I get off on people's fear. Girls' fear.

Ichabod bent to remove the boxers from around Joe's ankles then take off his socks. "Ye need tae learn when tae shut up. If ye keep backchattin' when the twins get here, ye'll only make it worse for yeself."

Flint glanced at the foot. "Ouch, I bet that hurts an' all."

"No comment."

Flint laughed. "I'm not a copper here, remember. I'm a fucking Cardigan, and don't you forget it."

"You're a joke, that's what you are." Joe sneered. "I bet you didn't even tell the twins you've been fucking about with me behind their backs."

"Why would I? They wouldn't have been able to interfere with a police operation on such a large scale. There's nothing I could have done to change what happened today, and they'd know that. I have my police job and this one. They're well aware I'm going to have to do things for work that I have no choice over."

Ichabod nodded. "Yeah, if ye weren't workin' for them when ye were told tae go undercover, they won't expect ye tae have said anythin', but if ye want my advice, from now on, if ye know Cardigan residents are up tae shit, tell them. *Or* if ye know they've been up tae shit in the past. I did the same last night, as it happens."

"What do you mean?" Flint asked.

"Someone told me somethin' they'd done years ago, before the twins took over, yet I informed them anyway. If in doubt, pass it on."

"Got it."

"If ye stay on the right side of them ye'll be grand."

"Uh, hello? I'm still here," Joe said, the arrogant prick.

Flint glared at him. "Listen to me, you little wankstain. You might think you're the be all and end all, but we don't. If we want to have a fucking chat over your head, we will, so shut your whinging cakehole."

Ichabod laughed. "I think I might grow tae like ye, Flint."

Mission accomplished. Get the right-hand man on side. "The feeling's mutual."

The door opened, and Flint stared that way. George strode in, the big bastard, the sight of him turning Flint's stomach over. Greg followed, then Hailey and who he assumed was Stacey, Hailey looking scared out of her mind, the other one with a mad glint in her eye—a woman scorned? Then someone else appeared, and Flint just about lost his breakfast. How the fuck was he going to get himself out of this one? He was going to have to lie through his teeth for however long this person was here.

He gawped. "Janine?"

Chapter Nineteen

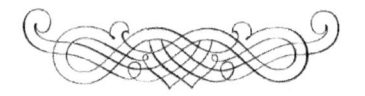

Janine never liked being called out on a Saturday, especially when it was her weekend off, but she couldn't resist this job. Seeing the shock on Flint's face was well worth leaving her boyfriend, Cameron, at home in front of the telly, her plans to laze about watching it with him pushed aside. She was brighter today, too.

Morning sickness had come and gone early, and she was almost like her old self. While she'd wanted to address Flint as soon as he'd seen her, she'd joined the others in putting forensic outfits on. It wouldn't hurt for him to wait for an explanation as to why she was here; he could stew for a bit. She'd quite enjoyed the thought of him shitting his pants on whether she'd come to arrest him, but he'd relaxed slightly as soon as Greg had handed her a protective outfit, showing she was in this shit just as much as everyone else.

"All of us put masks on except Flint." George eyed the copper. "I don't need to explain why, do I, mush?"

Flint shook his head. "No, I understand."

George, as usual, had to keep on turning the screw. "Just to be clear, filming you is for insurance. If you fuck us over, the video goes to your boss. Or maybe we'll get it played on social media so all your contacts know exactly who you are. We haven't done that before, but there's always a first time. Actually, killing you in a livestream would float my boat."

Janine smiled behind her mask.

Flint winced. "I get it."

Janine could well imagine how much strength of will it had taken for him not to stress the 'get' in that sentence. George had a habit of thinking people were dim, and he overexplained, although in this instance it was amusing. It had always rubbed her up the wrong way before, especially when it was directed at her, but she'd miss it when she finally hung up her Cardigan role. She'd agreed to meet up with Flint at some point for a few chats, tell him the score, and when she'd answered any questions and felt he knew what he was doing, he was on his own.

Janine walked towards Flint. She nodded in greeting.

"What the fuck are *you* doing here?" He glanced from her to George, then back to her.

"You're taking over my position, and if you ever think of opening that gob of yours and telling anyone at work what I've been doing, George will likely slit your throat—or do those things he just mentioned. So, how are you finding it so far?"

"Err, I haven't officially started. I'm only here because I was on a job for work. Undercover, so I shouldn't really be discussing it—no one outside of the team I've been working on can know I've had to let the cat out of the bag, okay?"

"Fine by me. The less shit I'm involved in the better. You can keep your little secret and shove it up your arse for all I care."

George laughed.

"Bloody hell, what the hell's your beef with me?" Flint asked her. "You've always given me weird looks at work."

"Ignore me. Hormones."

Let him think she was on her period. She hadn't told her boss she was up the duff yet, so she wasn't about to inform Flint before her DCI.

She'd been snarky with Flint because, despite wanting to hand her job over to someone else due to her pregnancy and the sheer stress working for the twins brought, she was irrationally jealous. She'd brought this change about, she'd picked Flint, sensing he was iffy beneath that friendly façade he adopted at work, yet she felt pushed out, which didn't make any sense. Contrary cow. She'd made this role truly her own, she had a system, her own way of doing things, and Flint was going to come in and do things his way. But she had to give up this need for control, it was ruining her life.

"Did you put my name forward?" Flint asked her.

"Yep."

"Why?"

"Because I knew you were bent."

Panic flared on his face, his upper lip dotted with sweat. He looked ridiculous with the suit hood's elastic digging into his skin, seeming to push all the flesh into his cheeks. "How?"

"Call it a sixth sense from one dodgy copper to another. Don't worry, I doubt if anyone else has noticed it. You're Mr I'll Help Everyone at work, aren't you."

He frowned. "Why did you say that sarcastically?"

She shrugged. "Because I felt like it? Because I can?"

George laughed again. "Much as I'm enjoying this back and forth, we need to crack on. Flint, what the fuck were you doing following Joe?"

Flint paled. "Police work. I couldn't get out of it. They sent me undercover yonks ago to wheedle my way into the county line. I've been watching them for a long time."

"Did he know you were a copper?"

"Yep, I played it so I was the bribing type, telling him he had to pay me protection money so I wouldn't dob him in, then I forced more money out of him when I fed him information."

"What kind of information?"

"Whether the police planned to be in a certain area, and last night I told him the runners were being rounded up. It was today, but I said it was Monday. I saw him going into Hailey's and twigged he must keep his earnings there. Reckoned he was going to bolt so he didn't get arrested."

"Where does he keep the gear?"

"In a trap house."

"A what?"

Janine smiled. "It's a house drug pushers work from. It usually has a resident in it who's *persuaded* to let people come in and use it as a base."

Those like Joe and people above him distanced themselves from the actual goings-on, using runners and the trap house resident so they took the fall should the police discover the line. It was a sneaky yet effective way to claim innocence if the shit hit the fan.

"Where is it?" George asked Flint.

"Kitchen Street, the first boarded house, but it's empty, no tenant. I've been there, just enough drugs stored at one time for the night's sales. There's a safe upstairs. His boss has a lock-up where the majority is kept. My advice would be to leave both locations well alone. My colleagues are aware they exist, and you don't want your fingerprints all over the gaff for them to find."

Janine waited for George to explode. *Three, two, one, go…*

"Do you think we'd be stupid enough not to wear forensic suits and gloves, you fucking div? Or even go there in the first place when we know the pigs are due? I mean, it's not like we don't know what we're doing, is it? Jesus fucking wept, what an utter prick. People like you really naff me off."

Interesting, when George was guilty of dishing out obvious advice himself. But then he always had picked fault in others when he committed the same infractions. He could do it, but no one else could, a trait she'd never liked in him.

Or myself.

"Sorry," Flint said. "I was just saying—"

George hand-chopped the air as though he wished he was cleaving Flint's head in half. "I've grown to hate that phrase. It's overused. Don't say it again if you value your bollocks." He stomped over to the man in the chair. "And as for you, *Joseph*. My God are we going to have fun. Greg's going to film it all so our shiny new copper is caught on film. How does it feel to be the star of the show, eh?"

Janine watched Flint for his reaction. The man slouched in defeat—had he thought he'd get away without an initiation?

"He's already fucking stabbed me in the back," Joe said.

"Metaphorically or literally?"

"Literally."

George glanced over at Flint. "What are you doing, damaging the goods before I get my hands on him?"

"He tried to escape. Headbutted Ichabod in the nuts and made for the tools on that table. I had to stop him."

Ichabod pointed to Joe's foot. "And I did that. The fecker tried tae get away at Hailey's."

George stared at Joe. "What part of 'I've been shot in the foot so I'd better not try to get away again' didn't you understand, you piss-flapping munter?"

"Aww, fuck you," Joe sighed out.

Janine recognised a man who knew he'd come to the end, and Joe had reached it. Then again, some of them got a second wind once the torture started, desperate to save their lives. She reckoned he belonged in that category because he had that way about him so many younger people did, in her experience. They thought the world owed them.

She walked over to him. Studied the man to get his measure.

He glared up at her, hatred in his eyes. "Who the fuck are you?"

George made a move to clout him one, but Janine held up a hand.

"I'm DI Janine Sheldon. Who the fuck are *you*? Apart from being so shit at what you do you ended up getting caught."

"People will have noticed I've disappeared already. They'll be out looking for me."

"I really couldn't give a single flying fuck about that. Someone else will be found to take your place by tonight. No one will *care* where you are come tomorrow. It'll be like you never existed."

She waited for a sour rebuttal, but it seemed he chewed on what she'd said.

"It's tough when you realise no one will miss you, isn't it?" She should know. The only person who'd have missed her when she'd been locked in a basement flat as a teenager would have been her mother, but only because she didn't have someone there to clean the house and do the washing, get some shopping in.

She thought about her dream to go to uni, how it had been snatched away from her, and vowed her child would never have their dreams ruined. She'd never expect them to be a skivvy while she drank herself to death and shagged umpteen men.

A bitter memory scored her mind's eye, and she had the need to kill this bastard for what he'd done, but that pleasure didn't belong to her. "I've heard about what you did to these women here. I went through rapes, I was abused, mind-fucked, so I know exactly how they feel. The least they deserve is an apology. What have you got to say for yourself?"

Joe sneered. "I'm not answering any of your questions. Women need to put up and shut up."

George punched him in the face, an uppercut right under his nose. The chair toppled back, and Joe's head whacked on the floor. Blood pissed out of his nostrils, and he growled, a wounded animal clenching his fists, his booby trap the rope around him instead of a hunter's steel jaws.

What must it feel like to be surrounded by so many people when you were naked and strapped to a chair, some of your sins inside the heads of everyone present? It didn't sound like he had any remorse, and his views on women were disgusting and archaic. Janine had met so many like him in her time as a copper—*and before, don't forget that flat*—and she had the sudden need to give it all up, to walk away from the degenerates, the killers, those who hurt others for fun. Do something else like youth work, make a difference elsewhere.

She no longer envied Flint but pitied him. He was going to see and do so many repulsive things for the twins. He'd question his sanity, feel trapped, wish he'd never set eyes on those two identical men who had the ability to shit the life out of you while smiling to your face.

But she loved them, she could admit that now. They'd become family.

She stood in front of Flint. "Do as you're told, don't think you can play them, because you can't, and everything will be fine. Step out of line, and you'll soon see what you get. Oh, and if you ever hurt my brothers, I'll fucking kill you myself."

She walked off to sit on the sofa, her eyes burning.

Fuck George and Greg for making her care about them.

Chapter Twenty

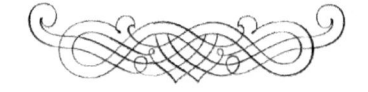

Pete hadn't died, but he'd had a stroke during the night by the looks of it. He breathed heavily, panicking, staring at her, and from the light coming in from the landing, she swore his face drooped on one side. Drool dribbled out of the corner of his lopsided mouth, glistening, and it churned her stomach.

Why was she still here? Why hadn't she walked out years ago, before that week at Belinda's? If not for her stupid need for revenge which had consumed her life as much as the abuse, she would have. She'd have taken Joe while he was still lovely and innocent, and he wouldn't have turned out the way he had. So was that her fault? It had to be. Her decision to remain in this marriage meant she'd allowed her son to become corrupted. Oh, she'd tried to fix the wrongs, teaching Joe different, but it hadn't worked. Then she'd just let it all happen, sinking into a world of violence, all the fight going out of her. When she'd woken up, courage burning inside her, it had been too late to fix things.

Pete moaned, trying to lift a hand, but it wouldn't move, so he picked it up with the other by the wrist, clearly trying to express what was wrong. He pleaded with her using his eyes, which held terror and uncertainty, the first time she'd ever seen him afraid.

Yeah, be afraid, you bastard. See what it feels like.

He tried to speak, but no words came out.

The air, rancid with the smell of his shit, had her battling against a heave, not to mention that drool stream growing even longer, snaking down his neck to pool in the hairs on his chest. She had to walk away so went over to snap the curtains apart and open the window. The crisp spring air wafted in, and she stuck her head out, gasping. He groaned behind her, but she ignored him, digesting this 'stroke' of bad luck—she smiled at the pun despite the need to scream. Maybe this was for the best. Maybe her guardian angel was listening after all. Pete becoming non-verbal was a godsend.

She pulled her head in, sniffed the bedroom and deemed it safe to breathe. At his bedside, she looked down at him, head tilted.

"What's the matter with you?" she asked briskly, seething that he wasn't dead—again. He had more lives than a fucking cat.

"St... St...ro...ke?"

"What was that?"

"Sttt...roke."

"Stop being so disgusting. I never want to stroke you again." How wicked of her to enjoy this, tormenting him, but she couldn't help herself. "Sex with you is the last thing on my mind."

"Pl...eas..."

"Please what?"

"He...lp me..."

"Help you to what? Have another shit? I've told you before, get yourself out of bed. The doctor said if you don't move, you'll seize up."

"Pooed...myself."

"You've crapped the bed? That's a shame. Right, I'll go down and make my breakfast. Going by the state of you, you won't be able to manage any. Your mouth's all wonky."

She walked from the room, smothering her laughter, a tiny bit of guilt poking at the part of her brain where empathy used to be. She should help him, he was seriously fucked, but it was six a.m., and if she left him until eight, there was a risk his brain might really *fry because he hadn't received medical help. He could die if she didn't phone for an ambulance, then all this would be over bar having Joe in her life.*

She made herself egg on toast and a cup of strong coffee, then sat and ate a leisurely breakfast. Fuck Pete, he could go without. Joe wouldn't be back until tomorrow—he'd texted late last night to say he was staying over again—and so there was no one to know she was ignoring her ill husband on this lovely Saturday morning.

Why hadn't the overdose worked?

She contemplated whether she'd gone mad, that his abuse had touched her brain so much that she failed to give a single fuck that he was suffering.

Breakfast went down well, and by the time she'd finished, the wash cycle she'd put on when she'd got up had completed. She hung it on the line, taking her time, colour-coding the pegs because Pete preferred that, then, in a fit of rebellion, she mixed them all up because she could—he had no say in what she did now. With another coffee, she sat at the plastic patio table and listened to the birds, then Roger shouting at their cat, Pru, for shitting in his vegetable patch.

"You've gone and done it all over the place, you filthy baggage," he moaned. "Psst! Get away. Go on, piss off."

Could Pete hear him through the open window? Did he want to call out to his friend but couldn't? The idea of him being so helpless pleased her—she'd *been helpless before she'd grown a set of balls, so it served him right to feel the same way. She watched the washing flapping in the breeze, the snap of a T-shirt bringing on thoughts of her snapping Pete's neck. Breaking his nose again like those thugs had done to him. Cracking another rib.*

Her next door's hinges creaked where she must be coming out to feed the birds. She did that every morning without fail, a huge lover of nature, and the scent of bacon fat wafted over the six-foot wooden fence. The woman put oats in the fat and made them into balls, then threw them on her grass. If she was such a lover of nature she'd put them high up on string, because Pru regularly enjoyed stalking the birds and taking them home to Belinda half dead.

Pete's groan had Amy shooting to her feet. He must have recognised the familiar sound of those hinges, so he couldn't be that fucked up by the stroke. Amy ran inside, locking the door, and rushed upstairs to shut the window. The neighbour glanced up, nosy cow that she was, and Amy waved. After all, she could claim she hadn't noticed Pete's droopy face until she'd shut the window and turned to look at him. Which she did now.

"I suppose you want me to call an ambulance," she said.

"Ya..."

Amy could say the stroke had happened later, the neighbour wouldn't be any the wiser. She could wait for a bit longer to see if it was one of those bad ones that killed you. She sighed, thinking of what she could do in the meantime. A bit of ironing perhaps. Get the hoover out.

Pete suddenly shook, his good arm flailing, and she stared while he convulsed, his eyes rolling. Panic gripped hold of her — actually seeing him die wasn't as fun as it had been when she'd imagined it. Her blood ran cold, and she got the shakes. Automatically, she took her phone out of her pocket and dialled nine-nine-

nine, wishing she didn't have to, but it seemed Pete hadn't beaten all the goodness out of her after all.

She left the room, closing the door so she didn't have to see the state of him.

Hopefully, he'd snuff it before help arrived.

Amy Googled two words the doctor had mentioned. May as well while she waited for more news from the specialist. They'd been here for three hours already, and tests had been done. Pete had suffered two strokes. The one in the night was ischemic, and the website informed her it was when a vessel was clogged and stopped the flow of blood to the brain. It was thrombotic, caused by a clot, likely because of the fight. According to the stats, eighty-seven percent of people suffered from those and had a good recovery rate.

Bollocks.

The weird convulsing was him having a haemorrhagic stroke, only thirteen percent likely, a ruptured blood vessel, and the severe symptoms got worse fast. If she hadn't phoned the ambulance he could have died, but as it was, he might be looking at permanent brain damage. Just what she needed. If he lived, a long road lay ahead of him. Physical, occupational, and speech therapy. She'd derive a warped source of pleasure from seeing him rely on her.

The doctor returned to the family room, giving her a sympathetic look. "He got lucky. You phoned us just in time. Another hour and…"

Bloody great. I thought that, didn't I? I said to wait until eight.

She wanted to scream. "Oh, thank God."

"There's a lot of recovery work to do, and I'm afraid he may have a change of personality, but it appears he'll pull through. He'll stay in here for a while, then go to a rehabilitation centre, then you'll be able to care for him at home."

She didn't want to care for him, she wanted to do what Belinda had said, put a pillow over his face and sit on it, but for now, she'd act the caring wife. "What sort of personality changes?"

"Aggression, a short temper due to the frustration of not being able to function as he once did."

So what's new?

The doctor continued. "Despite having two types of strokes, he can get better with medication, so I hope that puts your mind at rest. A change of diet. He has high cholesterol and also high blood pressure, so he'll be on medication for that as well. I think it's a combination of the attack on him and his underlying medical conditions. Has he ever told you he feels stressed?"

"No more than the usual person. He did say everything tasted salty, but that's no surprise. He likes to add it to his food." If Pete said otherwise, she could put it down to the strokes, that he was confused, didn't know what he was saying.

"I see. That explains the sodium. We took blood samples. It also seems he overdosed on his pain medication. There wasn't enough to kill him, though there may be some damage to his liver. Were you aware he'd taken so many?"

"What? No! They're on his bedside table. I wouldn't have thought to check them because he was capable of administering them himself. I was too frightened by the state of him this morning to have done anything other than ring the ambulance."

"Has he expressed a desire to harm himself?"

"Yes, last night actually."

"Yet you left the tablets within reach?"

"I didn't think he'd actually do it. I told my neighbour about it because it upset me so much. He went to sleep, so I popped round there to get some advice. Oh God, the attack…it must have affected him more than I thought. Is there anything I can do?"

"No, he's sleeping. Unless you want to sit with him, then I suggest you go home. It's pointless you being here if I'm honest."

"Okay. We have a son, so..."

"Then go. He's in safe hands. We'll call if there's a change or we think you need to come in."

"What does that mean?"

"If he has another stroke. You'll want to say goodbye if it appears it's going to be fatal."

She closed her eyes, faking that she couldn't handle this, but hope sprang up that even though they'd already started him on medication, he could still die. "Okay. If everything turns out all right, I'll pop by tomorrow morning."

Amy took a cab to the laundrette and burst inside, in need of Lil's calming influence and advice on what the hell to do next. A couple of customers glanced up from their phones to gawp at her, and she wanted to shout at them to mind their own fucking business, she was having a bloody crisis here!

Lil gaped at her. "Where's the sodding fire?"

"We need to talk out the back." Amy went behind the counter and into the staffroom. She plonked herself

down at the table, gripped the sides of her hair, and screeched out her frustration. Tears burned, and she choked on a sob. This had all gone so wrong. If she believed in God, she'd think he was stepping in every time Pete looked close to dying, preventing her from gaining freedom.

Lil came in and sat by her, holding Amy's hands. "What the fuck's gone on now*?"*

"I did what we discussed, with the tablets, and it didn't fucking work.*"*

Lil's eyes widened. "What?"

"He only went and had two strokes instead."

"Jesus Christ. Is he dead? Please tell me he's dead."

"No, the bastard's still alive. I called the ambulance just in time, apparently. If I'd waited another hour, he'd likely not be here. Why didn't I wait? For fuck's sake, I'm so stupid!"

"You're not, love. I expect your morals kicked in and that's why you picked up the phone."

"No, it was because he was having this weird fit and I panicked." Amy shook her head. "I shouldn't even be saying these things. I'm not normal to be so obsessed with him dying."

"You are."

"What?"

"Loads of women become obsessed. It's because it's the only thing they can control in situations like yours. Their thoughts are their own, sometimes the only *thing of their own, and it leads to this kind of scenario where you want him dead. I'd want him dead in your shoes, so don't you go feeling bad."*

"I don't, that's the problem, I'm just pissed off because now I'll be stuck with someone who can't function properly, I'll have to look after him. Then there's Joe to think about."

"You could leave. Loads of kids care for a parent when they're ill. He's old enough."

Amy snorted. "Come on, I can't see Joe doing that, can you?"

"But why should you *do it? You've been beaten up for years. Just because Pete's ill now, doesn't mean you have to stick around, all that 'What will the neighbours say?' bollocks. Who cares what they say?"*

"It would mean walking away from the house, my share of the equity, unless I can get him to sell it."

"Isn't that worth it?"

It should be, but it wasn't. It was true what Amy had said, she was *obsessed—with getting her due. But maybe she should cut her losses. Pack her clothes and personal belongings and leave once Pete was out of hospital. Amy could offer for Joe to come with her, and if he refused, let him suffer. He hated her, and if he loved his father so much, he could be stuck with him.*

She thought of the little boy he'd once been, and her eyes prickled. But that was in the past, she couldn't change it. Crying over what could have been wouldn't make a difference, it was a waste of energy and emotions.

"I'll see how things go," she said. "Maybe I'll walk away after all."

"He might have a fatal stroke in the meantime."

Amy grimaced. Chance would be a fine thing.

Chapter Twenty-One

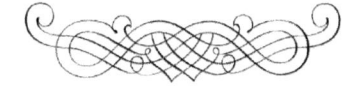

Upright again, the back of his head killing him with pounding throbs, the rope chafing his back wound, his bastard foot painful, Joe glared at Hailey who stood behind George to one side.

"What are you staring at, you stupid fucking slag?" He may as well go down verbally fighting, even if he got another punch to the face. Earlier, a sense of defeat had overcome him, but fuck it. He was going to die, he knew it, so he'd say whatever the hell he liked.

She stared back, a bit of defiance creeping into her expression above the mask. When she'd arrived, she'd looked afraid, and he'd thought—hoped—that she was here in the same capacity as him: to be bollocked by the twins for knowing what he did to earn a crust and not telling them. He'd soon been disabused of that notion, she was with them to see him suffer, putting on a forensic suit had proved that, so he'd put it down to her being a scaredy-cat bitch because she was going to witness his murder.

Fucking diddums.

"I'm not a slag," she said, calm, as though the words didn't hurt her. "I've only ever been with you and Riley, but so what if I was one? It doesn't give you the right to treat me like shit."

"I can treat you however I like. You're a woman, so fair game."

He waited for another punch from George, but it didn't come. Maybe it was Hailey's turn to take the floor now. Flint's predecessor had already had a pop, plus Flint, the Irish twat, and George, so he reckoned Greg would have a go, too, and Stacey.

Hailey shook her head. "How didn't I see who you were?"

"Again, you're a woman. Thick as mince, so you only see what you *want* to see—a happy ever after with your prince."

"I saw what you *let* me see. You weren't an arsehole to begin with."

"Err, that's the point. You start off nice until you've got them good and proper, then put down rules."

"I'm glad I found out who you really are."

"Why? It wasn't like you finished with me after, was it." He smirked. "Oh yeah, you were going to run away, except I stopped you. Why didn't you piss off after I'd left?"

"Because I met Stacey, and we planned to kill you."

He laughed. "I'd have liked to see you try."

They must have bottled it and gone to the twins instead.

He was curious what that bloke's name was, the one who'd grassed on him to Hailey. She never had said, saying she didn't know, he was a stranger in the pub. Joe had been stupid, bragging to a few mates from years back about running a line. It could have been any of them.

Nah, the Cribs lot are solid.

He shook his head at himself.

I should have kept it to myself.

His ego had taken over, though. He'd wanted to be the tough kid he'd been in school, the leader of the Cribs. It had annoyed him that they'd drifted apart when he'd thought they'd be tight for life.

"Who told you about me?" Joe asked, although he didn't expect her to tell him. Maybe she'd want to keep it to herself to maintain control. "You said you didn't know him, but I don't believe you."

"Him." She jerked her head at Flint.

Now Joe hadn't expected *that*. But then again, he should have. Flint had lied to him all along. But why had he informed her about him? What was his objective? The point? What had he got out of it?

George's eyebrows hiked up, and he seemed to view Flint with new eyes.

Flint aimed a smug smile Joe's way. "I warned her to keep away from you. Couldn't stand to see her get caught up in your shit when she was nothing to do with it. She's got a little boy who doesn't deserve to have a scrote like you in his life."

"Admirable," George said. "Nice of you to look after two of our residents."

Flint puffed up. Pride? His self-esteem inflating? God, what a pathetic tosser he was, so eager to please the twins, to be patted on the head like the dog he was.

"It wasn't right, her getting dragged into it," the copper said.

Joe grinned. Made eye contact with Hailey. "If you hadn't listened to him, you wouldn't have had to pack that suitcase." He paused. Grinned wider. "You wouldn't have been raped. *That was all your fault.* You brought it on yourself."

She lunged for him, her eyes full of spite and anger, hands raised, those sharp nails of hers ready to score his skin. Instead, she slapped, catching his sore nose, whacking and whacking him, grunts coming out of her in animalistic bursts. Happy he'd riled her, he clenched his fists, kept his eyes open to watch the hurt in hers, getting a kick out of it like Dad must do when he clouted Mum. His eyes watered—she'd caught his nose again—and the skin beside hers crinkling, perhaps from a smile, told him she thought she'd made him cry. That he was *sorry*.

Fuck. Off.

She stepped back, and the sting from her slaps joined the pain from his nose, back, and foot. He almost wished Ichabod had shot him in the kidney and he'd bled out before everyone else had arrived. But then the pain lessened a little, enough for him to channel his mind into pretending it wasn't there.

She bent over to hiss in his face, "I hate you, you sick bastard."

"Good," he spat back and loved the way she flinched.

She's still scared of me, even when I'm tied up.

She shook her head. "I don't get you at all."

"You were never supposed to. It's always been a game of me fucking with your head, right from day one, only you were too naïve to spot it."

Was she smiling again? What did she have up her sleeve? He schooled his features so they didn't betray him if she said something that angered him.

She straightened and folded her arms, but it didn't come off as a defensive move, nor did it seem as if she comforted herself. "Does it fuck with *your* head that me and Stacey are going to split all your money?"

You absolute pair of slags. It did fuck with him, but he'd never let her know that. The idea of those two jetting abroad on his dime, wasting it on makeup and clothes, Jesus… "Why would it? It's just payment for the slappers you are, although saying that, the amount of money there is, it would mean you were high-end tarts, and neither of you are any good in the sack to warrant that amount of cash."

She ignored that. It didn't seem to bother her at all. "I heard you do that. Pay women for sex."

He smirked. "Better get yourself checked out. I could have passed AIDs and all sorts on to you."

It was clear she'd already thought of that, herpes at the very least. Worried about it. Had perhaps shoved it to the back of her mind, something to deal with later, and he'd just reminded her that she might have some nasties festering down below because the last time he'd fucked her, he hadn't bothered with a condom. The thought of her scuttling to see her doctor tickled him, as did her shame at having to explain why she was there.

"Did you ever love Delaney like you said?" she asked.

What a stupid cow. Did she *want* him to hurt her feelings? "What, that spoiled, entitled, bastard kid of yours?"

She winced.

Another fist connected with Joe's jaw, this time from Flint, likely playing for Ichabod's camera, for the twins. "*Don't* say fuck all about her boy, got it? He's innocent in all this, like she is."

Joe laughed, agony spearing into his gum where he had a dodgy, rotting tooth. "Innocent? Nah, he's a cunning little sod. Knows exactly how to play his mum. I could have moulded him into a mini me. I'd have had him punching her in no time, given the chance."

Hailey chuffed air out. "How? You were barely there lately." She looked at George. "I think I need a knife now."

Oh fuck. So they'd had a discussion on the way here about a shiv, had they? Seemed like the ante had been upped and the real pain was about to begin.

Joe thought about Dad being angry over his death, gunning for whoever had murdered him. He wouldn't rest until he'd found out who'd done it. But would Joe's body ever be found? He doubted it. And Galaxy was going to do his nut. No product bagged up on the busiest night of the week. No one answering the main line burner. All those people already getting frustrated because he hadn't replied to anyone and sent gear their way since before he'd gone into Hailey's. He'd switched the phone off, needing a bit of peace while he'd climbed in the loft. There was no other way for the druggies to get their fix unless they approached other sellers on corners. The line runners might let Galaxy know something was up. They hadn't been sent out to deliver for a good while, and he hadn't arranged for couriers to do any drop-offs to restock.

What was the point in worrying about all that, though? It didn't matter anymore.

While he'd been stuck inside his head, George must have gone and picked up a knife. Hailey stood in front of him with it, her blade hand shaking.

Joe smiled.

She didn't have the balls.

Chapter Twenty-Two

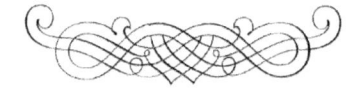

Hailey worried she didn't have the balls for this. She'd been right to abandon the plan and ask the twins to take over. Deliberately hurting someone more than she just had in her violent outburst—could she do it now push had come to shove? She recalled the pain of Joe carving her wrist, how he'd pinned her arm up to do it. How cold the wall had been, and the feel of the poster's edge touching her hand, sharp, her inanely thinking she'd get one of those sore paper cuts that hurt for ages. How he'd known just how much pressure to apply so he didn't reveal bone.

How bad had Stacey's wound been? Deeper? Had she been his first woman to mark? Or was some other poor cow out there with a scar to remind her of her time with this arsehole? Joe was only twenty-two, but that didn't mean anything. He could have had countless girlfriends before Stacey, then in between her and Hailey. And those sex workers. Had he dared to get his knife out on them? If so, were they still too afraid to come forward because, although the narrative was that sex workers shouldn't be penalised or treated differently because of their chosen profession, she'd bet some police officers would blame them for getting hurt. "If you weren't on the street half-dressed, he wouldn't have approached you…"

She was surprised by how calm she'd been until she'd hit him. She supposed that was because, apart from hurting Delaney, he'd already done one of the worst things to her, so his words now, although they stung, didn't pinch as much as they would have before. Besides, she didn't want him to know he affected her, although she'd fucked up there by attacking him.

"Who else have you cut apart from me and Stacey?" she asked.

"Wouldn't you like to know."

George barked, "She would, actually, that's why she fucking well asked, sunshine."

He sounded so *arsey*. Was he struggling with his Hulk again? Was that why Joe was like he was, because he had one, too?

Don't try to find excuses for him.

"I think they deserve some of that money," Hailey said.

Joe's expression gave her the reply she wanted. There *was* someone else.

"At least let me find her, talk to her, so she knows she isn't alone." Too late, she'd revealed she needed him, that he was the only one able to give her that information. "Who is she?" she pressed in an attempt to sound aggressive.

"No one you'd know. We were kids. Teenagers."

Oh. She hadn't thought he'd give her anything, but maybe he wanted to crow. And it somehow made it worse, that a kid had suffered, that he, also a kid, had been deranged, even at that age, to do something so horrible. How had the girl hidden the cuts from her parents? Or had she told them, reported it to the police?

Flint walked over to stand beside Hailey. "What the fuck are you on about here?"

Hailey held out her wrist, the scabs showing the rhombus and J clearly. Flint frowned; he appeared properly confused, and his lips clamped tight.

"Six years ago," Flint said.

Whoever Joe had hurt *must* have told the police, then.

"Natasha Evans." Flint shook his head. "It's your gang tag. You belonged to the Cribs, didn't you?"

Joe appeared startled. "How the fuck do *you* know about that?"

Flint glared. "I'm a copper. Do you think that might have something to do with it, perhaps?"

Who were the Cribs? And since when had Joe belonged to another bloody gang?

"Cribs?" George said. "Who the chuff are *they*?"

Flint turned to him. "No one to worry about. They don't exist anymore. They were just some trumped-up tossers in school, thinking they were all that. Five of them. Natasha never said who'd cut her, just about the gang. She wouldn't reveal *any* of their names. Said the Cribs strutted round school like they owned the place. She was scared of them; most of the kids were."

The barb had hurt Joe, Flint basically saying the Cribs were nothing but pathetic little boys trying to act hard. The more that was revealed about Joe, the more she realised he'd hidden so much of himself from her. He must have always had a penchant for being bad if he'd joined a gang as a kid. Now she came to think about it, he'd skimmed over his past whenever they'd talked on those first dates. He'd told her he'd grown up in a good home—yet had never taken her to meet his parents—and had an average life, no skeletons. Had he wanted to hide an appalling upbringing? Was he ashamed of it? She, on the other hand, had opened up, telling him all about Riley, how she'd mourned him, and that any man she ended up with would have to accept she still loved her childhood sweetheart and always would. Joe had said that wasn't a problem, he understood.

God, she'd fallen for his lies so hard.

"Cribs for life!" Joe shouted.

It startled Hailey, the ferocity in his voice, the volume of it, the pride. He was so obviously still devoted to the group. Who were they? Did they meet up every now and then to chat about the old days?

"How do you know they're not anyone to worry about?" George asked.

Flint ran a hand through his hair. "Natasha said they packed the gang in soon after I went to the school to find out who they were."

"How the hell would *she* know?" Joe snapped. "She left, went to that posh boarding place. I went round her gaff, but they'd moved, so how could she find that shit out?"

"There *were* phones back then," Flint said. "She still had friends from your school. You lot were all mouth and no trousers, couldn't even keep a gang together."

"No copper came to the school," Joe said. "What are you even on about?"

Flint smiled. "Just because you didn't know about it, doesn't mean that visit never happened. Just think, I've been after you way before you even met me, I just didn't know it was you who'd cut Natasha. And now I do."

Joe laughed. "What are you going to do about it? Bribe me again? That money train has left the station, you dickhead."

"You still don't get it, do you?" Flint said. "I didn't *have* that money, so whether the gravy train has ended doesn't make any odds to me. I had to hand it in because I was on a job for the *police*. Get it into your thick skull that I was *always* setting you up."

"You're a wanker," Joe muttered.

"Ditto. Except you're going to be a dead one."

Hailey went down on her knees by Joe's right arm. The rope didn't cover his wrist, and although she had to touch him and she didn't want to, she had to pay him back for marking her, for putting a permanent reminder on her skin. *He'd* never have to walk around with that reminder, he'd be dumped in the Thames, George said, but that was okay. So long as he felt the pain of it, she didn't care.

She reached out and gripped his fist, shuddering at the contact—his skin had gone clammy with sweat, so was he scared beneath all the bluster? She hoped so. Everyone had a little child inside them, didn't they, despite being adults. She prayed he'd been reduced to five years old, a kid bricking it inside but pretending to be a big boy on the outside.

When did he get that tattoo done?

Her hand holding the knife wouldn't stop shaking, but maybe that was a good thing. It might hurt him more if the blade juddered. She drew the first upright line of an H, hesitant at first, then going deeper. She glanced up, expecting him to grimace, but it was as if he barely felt it. She shifted her attention back to his wrist and drew the second upright, deeper, the resistance against the metal—bone?—transferring into her as a dull pressure. It was vile, her gag reflex kicking in; how anyone could get enjoyment out of this she didn't know. She dragged out the middle line, right across the bone again, hard, the skin parting to reveal the white of it, blood pouring. It was so disgusting she had to hold back a gasp.

The sight of it churned her stomach, but she continued with creating the frame around her initial—not a rhombus but a circle. It represented her love for Riley and Delaney, unbreakable, and how she'd never let her spirit be crushed by a man again. She doubted anyone but Stacey would understand.

Hailey checked his expression again. He stared ahead, teeth clenched. Was he fighting not to show how much it hurt? It *must* have done, she'd definitely gone down to the bone, so how the hell was he able to hide it? He gazed down at her. His eyes had gone black, and it sent a shudder through her.

She couldn't look at him anymore. Couldn't *stand* him. He sickened her to the point she wanted to throw up. She shook her head at him, to tell him he was pathetic, then focused her attention elsewhere.

A small pool of blood had formed on the floor, droplets around it, starburst patterns on their edges where they'd hit the solid surface. Red continued to drip, meandering down his thumb, plopping off and adding to the puddle. She caught a waft of the smell. She wouldn't let him see her heaving, so she swallowed it down and got to her feet, needing to create space between them. Moving back, she stood beside Stacey who took her free hand and held it tight.

"Are you okay?" Stacey whispered.

"Yes and no."

Hailey experienced the rush of many emotions at once. Disgust at herself for cutting someone, even though he'd been a bastard to her. Sadness for it coming to this when she'd thought she'd been lucky enough to find another Riley—naïve enough, stupid enough. Anger at the lies, the manipulation, the verbal and sexual abuse. She'd never forget that time in Delaney's bedroom, every touch of his hand on her, the tightness of his grip on her wrists, the rasp of the quilt cover against her face, the smell of the washing powder on the duvet cover… In the future, she expected so many triggers to assault her, but at least she knew they were coming, so maybe it wouldn't hit her so hard.

Or maybe it would.

Perhaps she should shove it to the back of her mind. Try to move on as if it hadn't happened. Or she might take the twins up on their offer of free therapy. Do it sooner rather than later, while it was all so fresh. Put it to bed now instead of later down the line when she discovered it wasn't as easy to sweep it under the carpet as she'd thought. That it *couldn't* be swept under.

She asked herself if she'd done enough. Whether she should hurt him more. Feel the knife sliding into his stomach like she'd envisaged ever since she and Stacey had created their plan. She'd wanted to do that so much, but now… No, she'd rather let Stacey do it. At least her new friend *wanted* to.

George stepped towards them, his back to Joe. "You've had enough."

Hailey nodded, relieved the decision had been made for her.

Sometimes, it was better to let other people make choices for you.

Chapter Twenty-Three

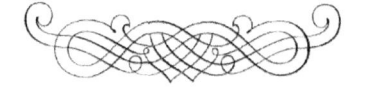

Stacey had harboured so much ill will towards Joe for so long that now the time had finally come to enact her revenge, she brimmed with the hatred she thought she'd buried. Yes, she'd had therapy, learning for forgive herself for falling for his bullshit, falling for *him*, but there had always been a loose end dangling—him not saying sorry—that no amount of couch sessions could tie a knot in. He hadn't even said it when her brothers, Diddy and Kaiser, had kicked the shit out of him. Joe had refused to atone for anything throughout the beating. He'd stayed out of sight while he'd recovered—Diddy and Kaiser and kept tabs on him—and when he'd eventually crawled out of his flat, he'd kept a low profile. Her brothers had backed off once it seemed their warning had worked.

Maybe they'd been arrogant to think Joe had listened to them, but arrogance might not be the right word. Of *course* you'd think someone would take your advice after you'd broken their bones and wrecked their face.

When Stacey had seen the cuts on Hailey's arm in Home Bargains, everything had come tumbling back, her whole body going cold because the lesson *hadn't* worked. In that moment, when Hailey had moved away as if to bolt, Stacey had wished Diddy and Kaiser had killed that bastard like they'd wanted to in the first place, only she'd begged them not to in case they'd got caught, sent down for murder. The guilt that Joe had gone on to hurt someone else would never leave Stacey, but at least she'd had the decency to apologise to Hailey about that. Not that Joe's actions were her fault—she needed to remember that; what *he'd* chosen to do wasn't on her. It still prickled her, though, that sense of being to blame.

And it turned out he'd done it to someone else before Stacey. A girl. She hoped he'd only cut her—although 'only' sounded like it could be dismissed as nothing much, and she didn't mean it like that. But it was better than the rest, the final humiliation being rape. She wanted to ask Flint whether Natasha had been through that ordeal, considering she'd moved school and house. Poor kid.

"Will you find Natasha, make sure she's okay?" she asked George.

"Yeah."

Joe stared at her, his lips twitching into that smirk she'd grown to hate when he'd transitioned from lovely boyfriend to verbal abuser to physical to sexual. He really did think he was something special, didn't he? The arrogance of him was almost palpable, an aura. And she'd bet he thought she was weak for caring about Natasha.

"Like what you see?" he asked.

No, she didn't, she despised it, couldn't believe she'd ever found him attractive, but she was going to try hard not to let him know how much he'd affected her in the past and still did. To do that would give him pleasure, ammunition. People like him fed off another's emotions, hoovered them up as fuel to boost their already ballooned egos.

"Are you going to say sorry to Hailey?" What she also meant was, "And to me?" But saying that would let him know she craved an apology, something she hadn't realised she'd wanted until today. But whatever apology she got from him would be hollow, forced out of him by torture, and it wouldn't be heartfelt. He wouldn't mean it, so what was the point in him giving her one?

"Am I fuck," he said. "Why should I when I'm *not* sorry? I enjoyed every fucking minute of it."

He was sick in the head. Just as bad as his father, someone she'd only met once, and that had been by accident in the Red Lion. She should have questioned that sooner, why Joe didn't want to take her round theirs; instead, she'd waited until after they'd walked away from his mum and dad to sit elsewhere.

"Is he always like that?" she asked.

"Yep. Can you see now why I didn't introduce you? He's a fucking monster," Joe said. "Treats my mum like shit. Did you hear what he said to her? 'Shut up and sit down, you stupid cow!'? I mean, who does that?"

Stacey swallowed it, thinking Joe had been created from a different mould, that he recognised speaking to a woman like that wasn't on, but even then a twinge had bothered her—him not standing up for his mother, just letting his dad say what he liked. Was Joe scared of him?

"Can't you help her get away from him?" she asked.

"There's no point. She's so used to it that she thinks it's normal. I can barely stand to go round there and see it going on."

"You could ring the police."

"Huh, fat lot of good they'd do."

Stacey had accepted that—God, she hated herself for that now, leaving that woman to suffer; where the fuck was her girl code? She'd suggested they leave the pub rather than have Joe feeling bad, knowing the monster was staring over at them, nodding and grinning at him. And now she knew why. His father had been congratulating him on snagging a stupid little cow who'd hung on his son's every word. The secret complicity of it, Stacey unaware, sickened her.

"How's your dad?" she asked.

Joe gave her a filthy look. "Don't talk about him."

"What, about the man who tried to mould a little boy into a replica of himself?"

"What do you mean, tried? He did!"

She'd come to that in a minute. "Doesn't it rile you up to know he manipulated you exactly the same way you manipulated women? What does it feel like to know you were weak, exploited, and there was nothing you could do about it?"

She'd hit a nerve. Joe tried to hide a flinch, but it flickered all the same. *This* was the way to hurt him, to get a reaction.

"You're as pathetic as I was—note I said *was*, because I'm over you, yet you're still dancing to his tune. You fell for whatever he said and did and likely still do. *You're* being controlled, whereas the only person controlling *me* is myself. What you did to me, it means nothing, because *you* mean nothing. You're insignificant."

A sneer carved into his spiteful face. "You're a liar. You're not over me. You can't be after what I did. You wouldn't be here if you didn't care."

"Really? You profess to be able to look into my mind and know how I feel now? That won't work anymore. All that gaslighting you did, making me think you *could* read my mind...once you see it in someone, you can see it in others a damn sight sooner. I've learned to spot people like you a mile away. You didn't break me, so you failed. You're not a patch on your dad. At least he's been able to control the same woman for years. Look at you, there's been at least me and Hailey you've done it to, and Natasha, maybe others—either your dad didn't teach you well enough or you're just a crap student."

"Shut the fuck up. I told you not to talk about him."

"Why, don't you like me tearing holes in your hero's cape? He isn't a hero, he's a fucking wanker and needs a kicking."

"That can be arranged," George said. "Actually, it *will* be arranged."

Joe glared at him. "Don't you *dare* touch my dad."

George laughed and looked around at everyone. "Hark at him. He thinks I'd listen to his orders." He cocked his head at Joe. "Haven't you learned anything, my old son? Didn't you pick up on the rumours about me and my brother? Or do you think you're so fucking special that the rules and punishments don't apply to you?"

"That sounds about right," Stacey said. "He's just a kid who hasn't grown up, thinks the world revolves around him."

"You're seriously naffing me off, Stace," Joe said.

She laughed. "That look, those words, they won't work on me. I'm not the person you think I am. I couldn't give a single *fuck* about you—your tactics on me didn't stick, so again, you're nothing like your father. You're not a carbon copy, you're just a pathetic loser trying to be one. Honestly, you're nothing but a waste of space. Oh, and you've got a small dick."

It was a lie, but it would piss him off.

Titters went round, and Joe fumed.

Hailey burst out laughing, a manic babbling brook of sound verging on hysteria. Stacey clutched her new friend's hand tighter, giving her support, because she could guess why she was laughing so much—the tension of all this, the memories. Laughter was better than sobs.

Hailey sobered. Wiped her eyes with her free hand and turned to Stacey. "Cut it off." She appealed to George. "Someone, anyone, cut the fucking thing off."

Flint stepped forward, raising his knife. He didn't slice across but stabbed downwards, right into the centre of the penis and through the bollocks beneath, the top if the blade meeting with the wood of the seat creating a dull thud.

Joe howled, and he'd *hate* that he hadn't been able to stay quiet. Everyone studied him, even Janine got up to stand in the row, a wall of observers who seemed to enjoy watching him in pain. Flint removed the knife, holding it up to Ichabod who aimed his phone at him. This was all being filmed, but Stacey didn't give a single shit, she had a mask on. And anyway, she wasn't about to tell anyone about today, she'd only ever talk to Hailey about it afterwards, and if it made the twins feel better that they had her on camera, whatever.

Flint joined the line, standing between George and Greg. It felt like a statement, him placing himself there. Although curious about the dynamics between the twins and the copper, Stacey cast it aside and walked over to the table behind Joe. So many things to choose from. A screwdriver caught her attention, and she picked it up in her gloved hand. If she stabbed it in his eye, she estimated the end of the metal would reach the back of his head if she put enough strength behind it. Would she be strong enough to penetrate his brain? She imagined what Diddy and Kaiser would think of her, their little sister, warped enough that she had no trouble envisaging attacking Joe. She'd hidden it from them, her latent anger, making out she was fine. And poor Chaz, he'd think she was evil if he knew what went through her mind now: Joe's eye popping; her carving a tunnel through the part of the brain that made him bad; blood sprouting; his screams.

She pulled herself out of the horror.

He'd shut up screeching now, but she'd bet his dick was agony.

Stacey took the screwdriver over to Joe and stood in front of him. Knowing the others were behind her stirred courage, although the anger she felt towards this piss-poor excuse for a man would carry her through. Tears ran over his cheeks, and he stared down at his ruined package, shaking his head, then raised it to catch sight of the screwdriver. A slight tic contracted beside his mouth, where he perhaps fought not to say something, to warn her not to dare use the weapon on him.

She didn't go for his eye. Instead, in a downwards arc, she stabbed him in the fleshy part of his thigh. He screamed again between gritted teeth, veins standing up on his temples, his face turning red. She twisted the screwdriver, waggling the handle to invite more pain to the party, and a little voice whispered that she shouldn't like this as much as she did, that she might have allowed herself to become unhinged.

That she still allowed his actions to control her.

True, but it was on *her* terms, *her* choice. She yanked the tool out and stabbed his thigh again and again, then moved to his neck. She rammed the metal into the side of it and stepped back, smiling at the yellow-and-black handle sitting against his skin, and if she pulled it out, blood would piss in a jetting pulse.

"My turn." Flint stepped forward and stood to the side of Joe, gripping his hair to keep his head still.

Joe sobbed, the pain must be unbearable, but Stacey sensed it would be all over soon. Too soon. She wanted him to suffer more.

Flint positioned the blade at one side of Joe's neck. "You were always meant to be mine."

He sliced across before Stacey had the chance to say she wanted to do it, the skin parting, gaping, blood sheeting out, down his throat and onto the top of his chest. It soaked into the rope, spreading through the top coil and sinking into the next. Flint sliced again, sawing back and forth. He wrenched the screwdriver out and tossed it away. Flint cut at the sides of the neck as if possessed. Joe spasmed, his fists shivering, and a breath gusted out of his mouth, more of a wheeze, a gurgle of claret following. His head dropped back, on a spine hinge, and now the rope was a bib of scarlet. His body stilled, twitched momentarily, and stilled again.

George stepped forward. Inspected the neck. "Nice work."

Flint nodded. "Cheers."

"Take him off that chair for me, someone," George said. "I've got a lot of anger to get out of me, and even though he's dead, I'll still enjoy kicking the shit out of him."

Stacey understood having anger inside you with no outlet. But she'd had one now, and while the rage still simmered, it was better than the beast she'd been carrying around with her, thinking she'd banished it. She glanced at Hailey, who stood with Janine's arms around her, her face pressed to the woman's chest. The enormity of what had happened here had clearly struck her, and thank fuck they hadn't gone to Kitchen Street on their own to stab Joe there. Hailey would have bottled it, and the delay would have meant he'd have got the upper hand before Stacey could take the knife off her and launch it into him. It was one thing to imagine doing it and believing you could, but when it came down to the wire, Hailey had caved under pressure.

Stacey turned. Flint had untied Joe and dragged him onto the floor, the knife discarded nearby. He moved back and picked it up.

"There's a bucket over there," George said. "Put the screwdriver and knife in it." He smiled down at Joe. "*Now* you can come out to play."

It took a moment for Stacey to realise he wasn't speaking to the dead man but to himself. That mad Hulk thing who lived inside him.

And then he swung the first kick.

Chapter Twenty-Four

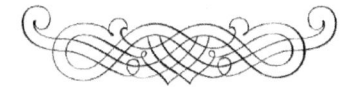

Years had passed since Pete's strokes, and Amy was still there, waiting for the day he had another one, or maybe a heart attack from all the burgers and crap she cooked him for dinner while she ate healthily. He had double helpings, and she imagined all that fat building up as cholesterol, but each time he had an annual checkup, his meds were upped and he was told

to cut the crap out of his diet. He never did, asking for more of the same, and she was convinced he was addicted to homemade fast food. Maybe the part of his brain that regulated addiction was broken.

Joe, twenty-two now, had moved out three years ago, thank God, living in a rented flat. At least there was half the verbal abuse, unless he came round for a visit, which wasn't often. He preferred to meet his father in the Red Lion, likely bitching about her. What a crap mother she'd been. How rude she was to persuade Pete, while he'd still been confused, to let her have his savings to pay for a carer to come in twice a day while she worked at the laundrette. Pete had told her this one night after a bellyful of booze, going off on a rant. His brain had skipped over events a lot in the early days, and he'd brought things up months or years later, as though they'd only just been discussing it.

The doctor had been right. Pete's personality had *changed, or, to be more precise, his original one had got worse. To begin with, after he'd come out of the hospital, he'd shouted at her instead of speaking—he'd been incapable of normal-volume speech, his words slurred, and she'd wondered if his hearing was affected. He'd thrown things, some of them striking her, one episode resulting in a broken nose as a plate had smacked into it, side on.*

Of course, everyone excused it because of the strokes. God had played a blinder, giving Pete the perfect excuse to treat her badly and get away with it.

Back then, he couldn't remember that conversation they'd had the night she'd recorded it until she'd reminded him, nor could he recall the majority of their marriage—the strokes or a convenient way for him to make out he wasn't culpable? Some of his memories had been completely wiped, him staring at her, dumb as fuck, or he remembered them wrong.

To rewind time to when they'd first got together, she'd tried to create a new, fake past for them, telling him stories of how much they'd been in love, her way to get him to latch on to them and become the man she'd told him he'd been, but Joe had said otherwise, sitting by his dad's bed and feeding him the truth, one horrible incident at a time. Pete had retained his spiteful streak and had laughed. Funny, but not fucking funny, how he hadn't forgotten his views on women.

He still hadn't had the gap between his teeth fixed.

Mum had refused to come round after one exceptionally horrid visit. Pete had behaved how he did with Amy, and her parents had seen it for the first time. Dad had said the stroke must have changed him, to cut Pete some slack because he couldn't help it, but Mum seemed to sense what had really been going on all those years, giving Amy one of her penetrating stares: Why didn't you tell me?

Dad had popped in a few times after that, then didn't bother. Pete's parents dropped in while Amy was at work, so at least she hadn't had to put up with listening to Orla pandering to her son the way she always did, thinking her boy could do no wrong. He'd once called her a cow, and she'd said, "There, there, it's the nasty strokes' fault, making you say that."

Orla had died recently, cancer eating away at her, and Pete hadn't seemed to care. Joe had taken it badly, though, which had surprised Amy. She'd thought he didn't have it in him to cry.

She sat with her mother now, needing to confess, to get all these hideous thoughts and feelings out of her. She'd told Lil in dribs and drabs, but not every single thing. It was time to reveal everything, the burden had become too heavy. Dad had gone to the pub, and Amy had nipped into theirs after work.

"I didn't say it at the time, I kept my mouth shut because you had a lot on your plate, but that man's been hitting you for years, hasn't he." *Mum sipped her tea.*

How the hell did she know what Amy was going to say? And why had she waited until now to bring it up?

Amy nodded. "Yes."

"Why did you stay? Because of Joe? You could have taken him with you. Pete wouldn't have had a leg to stand on if you'd reported him for abuse."

"You don't know the half of it."

Mum paused with the cup halfway to her mouth. "What do you mean?"

"It's a lot messier than you can imagine."

"Tell me."

"So you **want** to see I'm not the perfect daughter you seem to think I am?"

"Listen to me, love. Like Pete's mum was with regards to her boy, I don't give a rat's arse what you've done, you'll always be my baby. Even if you committed murder, I'd stick by you."

"I almost did," Amy said on a borderline hysterical laugh. "And I'm not a patch on you or Orla because I **wouldn't** stick by my son."

Mum put her cup down and reached out to take Amy's hand. "Talk to me. Tell me why. Joe's got to have done something really bad for you to not want to bail him out."

Amy started from the beginning, and by the time she'd finished, Mum was crying. Amy, however, was dry-eyed. She had no more tears to shed.

"*All this time I could have helped you,*" *Mum said.* "*Oh, my darling, I'm so bloody sorry you went through this alone.*"

"*I wasn't alone, I had Lil and Belinda.*"

"*You know what I mean.*"

"*So do you think I need psychiatric help? I want to kill him, Mum, fucking* kill him, *and I hate my own kid. That's not normal. You've never seen Joe behave badly, but I'm telling you, that boy is an outright nutter. He scares me with how cruel he is. Those two know who to behave in front of, they know how to play the game. I got caught up in trying to win it instead of them, and it didn't work out. I became obsessed with revenge, and it all went wrong.*"

"*Now Pete's back at work, maybe you should think about leaving. Joe's not your problem anymore. I'll never get over what you've told me about that child, but I believe you, and if you say he's rancid, then he is. But life is passing you by with you wanting justice, and instead of truly living, you're existing in the hope your husband dies, for what, money? That doesn't always make you happy. What does Lil have to say about all this?*"

"She's been brilliant—don't think badly of her, will you, she was just trying to help me. But I think, if I'm going to move on, that I'll have to leave the laundrette. She brings it all up every now and again, suggests new ways to kill him, and because none of them are feasible, it's pointless discussing it. She's as obsessed as me if I'm honest, and it's not good for her, not fair."

"If I know Lil, no one can tell her what to do or how to feel. If she's helping, it's because she wants to."

"I know, but…"

"Look, we can pop into an estate agent and sort a flat. Me and Dad can give you the bond and first month's rent. There might even be some furnished ones. You need your own space, your own life. Get a solicitor to send Pete a letter saying you want the cash for your portion of the house. Take him to court for it if he refuses, force the bastard to agree to sell it. Let him wallow in his own hatred all by himself. Tell the police what he's done and take out a restraining order. I know they're not worth the paper they're written on and you'd have to be harmed before the police will do anything, but if you go down the legal route, it'll be him who gets in the shit if he breaches the conditions."

"But I still want him dead, Mum. I can't get it out of my head. Everything he did to me, it was sustained, violent, bloody awful, and he has to pay. If I'm with

him, he won't start again with someone else and ruin her, too."

"You can't stay with him because of that, love. You said about porn. Is he still watching it?"

"Yes, because I haven't let him touch me since the strokes. I can't stand him anywhere near me. I slept on the sofa while Joe was home, and now I'm in his old room."

"How have you got away with that if Pete's got such a bad temper?"

"Because of that recording. It's my insurance. If he does anything to me, he thinks Belinda will send it to the police."

"So he remembered that? You recording him?"

"Not at first, I had to tell him. He just stared at me blankly, like I was making it up, then the next day he mentioned it, as if his memory had been jogged. He got lairy, talking about all the sarky things I'd said to him that night—he even remembered the night before when I burned his stomach with curry."

"You did what?" Mum laughed.

"It was fucking brilliant, hurting him. Anyway, he raised his fist, and I had to remind him, again, about the recording. He's left me alone since, hasn't laid a hand on me, but he's still mentally and verbally abusive."

Mum sighed. "I know you, and you're going to stay with him, aren't you, until you get what you want?"

"He owes me. I want the life insurance."

Mum shook her head. "I also know I won't be able to talk you out of it. You're as stubborn as your father. I can't say I don't think it's a waste of your life because I do, but if it makes you feel better, do what you have to, but for fuck's sake, don't get caught." She paused. "You could go to The Brothers now Ron's dead — useless shit that he was, he wouldn't have had Pete killed because he was a bastard to women himself and would have patted him on the back. But George especially, he'd go apeshit over this. One word in his ear, that's all it would take. He'd be round yours like a shot."

"I don't want the twins to do it. I need to do it myself."

"Then ask them if you can. I'm sure they'd let you."

It was something to think about.

"I love you, Amy." Mum squeezed her hand. "Whatever you decide to do, I'm here, and your dad won't know about any of this from me, all right?"

Amy nodded. "I'm sorry I'm such a fuck-up."

"No, never. You're a product of that arsehole's control, and if I had the guts, I'd kill him myself."

Amy had another confession. "I'm on tablets. It's the only way I can cope."

"I'm not surprised."

"They're not working like they used to. I'm going to have to go to the doctor and get them upped."

"Do whatever you need to." *Mum sighed. Shook her head.* "Joe...it's all such a shock."

"I don't know what he's up to lately, he said he was on benefits, but he's never short of cash for the pub. He treats Pete there a lot. I'm now pinning my hopes on alcohol poisoning, liver failure." *Amy felt exhausted having spewed out her whole marriage to the one person she should have turned to from the beginning of it all, but she still had more to discuss.* "Do you remember Stacey?"

"That older woman Joe was seeing? The one we never met?"

"Yes. I saw her once. She came into the Red Lion when we were in there. First time we'd met her. Joe was doing his usual, like he's always done with you and Dad, making out he's sweetness and light. I wanted to punch his fucking lights out and tell Stacey to get away from him as fast as she could, but I was playing my part again, doing as Pete expected. He called me a few names in front of her, and the poor cow looked horrified. Anyway, however long down the line,

Joe came to ours all beaten up, and I mean proper beaten up. He said he'd been warned to stay away from Stacey by her brothers, they'd kicked him about, and do you know why?"

"Oh God, what…"

"He told me he'd raped her. Thought it was funny. So if you ever think about feeling sorry for him, remember that. He's monster like his father."

"Oh my bloody good God, that poor girl. Didn't she report him?"

"Seems not, and I didn't either—but I wish I had. He's seeing someone else now. She's got a little boy. Joe thinks I don't know, but I saw them together in town, they walked past Boots when I was in there getting my prescription. What if he…I mean, what if he does it to her?"

"Do you know anything about her, her surname, where she lives? Maybe you could go round and warn her."

"I know nothing except she's blonde. I'm worried about her son. What if Joe does the same as Pete did? Teaches the poor kid to be abusive?"

"You're stuck on this one, unfortunately. Let's hope she sees him for who he is and finishes with him."

"He could turn nasty if she does."

Mum shook her head. "Then we'll have to pray he doesn't, won't we."

Chapter Twenty-Five

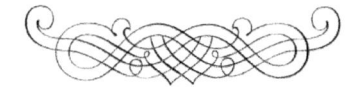

Galaxy read the message again, even though it was an hour old and he knew damn well what it said: WE HAVEN'T HAD ANY JOBS FOR TWO HOURS, J HASN'T CONTACTED US. He'd tried getting hold of Joe himself, had even paid a visit to his flat—no answer—and the trap house—tonight's drugs were still there. His third stop, the lock-up, had confirmed Joe hadn't banked yesterday's earnings in the safe. Galaxy knew he hadn't, he'd checked the camera recording first thing this morning, like he did every morning, and he planned to ream Joe a new arsehole about having the money in his flat overnight. He'd been warned about it before, and he now had to pay the price for ignoring the rules a second time.

Galaxy's machete was going to get an outing.

Where the fuck is he?

Could he have been abducted? That would explain why the drugs were still in the trap house. Had he been on his way to the lock-up last night and someone had jumped him for the money? No, that didn't make sense. The message had said no jobs for two hours, so Joe had clearly been working up until then. But he *could* have been nabbed after he'd sent the last text to a runner.

Galaxy entered the Red Lion. If he found him in here, he'd do his nut. Drag the twat out onto the street and give him a pasting, sod the CCTV cameras. Joe having a bevvy while fielding messages was fine, so long as no one saw his screen. If the work got done, Galaxy didn't give a toss, but seeing as it wasn't…

A quick scout round proved fruitless, and his anger grew. Flint wasn't in here either, so he must be working for the police this weekend. Were they together? Or had Joe fucked off with his saved earnings, plus last night's takings? Nah, surely he'd have taken the drugs from the trap house with him, which Galaxy currently had in his backpack along with a lightweight set of digital scales.

He checked the toilets, then poked his head out the back into the garden area. Two of his best customers sat smoking spliffs at one of the wooden bench tables, laughing insanely, probably high as kites.

He went over and sat opposite them. "Have you contacted Joe today?"

One of them waggled his joint. "Well, yeah..."

"Right, so you've had a delivery."

"Yep."

"What time was that?"

"About eleven? Something like that. Who are you anyway, and what do you want to know for?"

Galaxy didn't get involved with the punters himself anymore. Now he'd moved up the hierarchy, he didn't have to show his face. His days as a runner were over, and it had been a long time ago when he'd done that. He'd changed his appearance so no one would recognise him.

He left them to it and returned inside. Strutted up to the bar and asked the woman behind it, "Seen Joe Osbourne?"

"Not today, love, no."

Dogged off, he walked out. On the way home, he cursed Joe. Luckily, Joe's line burner messages replicated on other spare burners in Galaxy's safe, connected by an app that synced the texts across all devices. Google was a fucking smart company. As Galaxy had trusted Joe, he hadn't felt the need to keep up with those messages after he'd trained him, but he'd have to get a burner out and respond to requests for gear.

It was going to take him a while to get through them all, there were hundreds every day, plus there were the drugs to bag up for tonight. Joe going AWOL had fucked things up. It was up to Galaxy to become the line manager again—his old job—until he worked out which runner he'd pick to take Joe's place, because that little bastard was no longer welcome in the line.

He sighed, entering his place to collect the burner, then he'd go to the lock-up and do the bagging in between fielding messages. He was supposed to have been entertaining a lady later, and now he'd have to cancel.

FML.

Chapter Twenty-Six

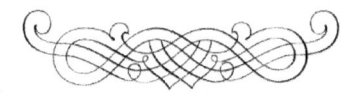

Flint had hated having to leave his forensic gear with the twins for them to supposedly burn all of the suits later, because he had a feeling *his* wouldn't be destroyed. As well as the video, which he was crapping himself about, they'd keep his outfit for extra protection. There was no way on this earth he'd be able to get out of being their copper now. Even if he went to work and made out to his senior officers that he'd been forced to take part in today, it wouldn't hold water. He'd been too keen to step in and stab Joe in the cock, to slice his throat, and that would be clear on the footage. No one would believe he'd just been acting.

So this was it. His life now. At their beck and call.

Maybe he'd grow to like it, but he'd definitely have to lump it.

As for Janine… He'd had no idea she was bent. Her frosty exterior and barked conversations at the station were a good cover for any stress she'd endured in her Cardigan role, whereas he'd opted to be Mr Happy, and his future stress would be hard work to hide. Still, he'd made his bed and had to lie in it.

Why is she leaving, though? And how come the twins are letting her go? Was it a requirement that she found a replacement before she'd be set free?

He'd been told he had to have a meet-up with her at some point, a kind of changing-of-the-guard chat, and to be fair, he appreciated she'd be helping him out. He had no idea how this worked—all he had was a brand-new burner and had been told to await instructions. He supposed, now he'd completed his initiation, that he might be called on sooner now. Or were they going to wait until Janine had said whatever she had to say? Was she going to train him?

He'd believed her when she'd said she'd kill him if he hurt her brothers. Not *The* Brothers, *hers*. What, was she like their sister or something? Had she been working for them for so long that she was considered part of their family? Would he be pulled into the fold to that degree in the end?

He'd come home and put the clothes he'd had on under the forensic suit on a hot wash cycle, and his trainers, adding Ace bleach to the detergent drawer with the washing powder. Despite all that blood and the nasty stink of it still lingering up his nose, he hadn't been put off eating. He'd seen many a vile thing at work anyway, so he had a strong stomach. He'd made toasted sandwiches and now sat in front of his perv laptop.

He bit off a corner of a sandwich, the cheese too hot inside, burning his tongue. But a scalded mouth was the least of his worries. Seeing Hailey's scabs had all but unravelled him, and he was surprised he'd kept it together as well as he had. The sight of them had zipped him right back to the past where he'd seen the same on Natasha's arm after she'd shown him a picture on London Teens.

He scrolled to her file where he kept the entirety of their conversations in screenshots, plus her innocent images. He found the part where she'd told him what had been going on and smiled at the name he'd used with her: Boy_with_a_Job. The girls had come flocking when he'd logged on with that one, thinking he had money to spend on them, but he'd only chosen her.

Wonder_Teen: Can I tell you something?

Boy_with_a_Job: Yep.

He'd thought she was going to say she'd ditched her boyfriend, something he'd been trying to get her to do for a while, subtly pointing out that some of the things the lad said to her, things she'd passed on to Flint, weren't exactly nice.

Wonder_Teen: You know that boy I've been going out with?

Boy_with_a_Job: Yeah…

Wonder_Teen: He cut me last night. [Sad face]

Boy_with_a_Job: What? [angry face] Have you told your mum and dad?

Wonder_Teen: No. I can't. [crying face] He'll cut me again, he said so. He's in a gang. Sorry I didn't tell you that bit before.

Boy_with_a_Job: What's his name? I'll come to your school tomorrow. Me and my mates will do him over.

Wonder_Teen: I can't say. He'll know I grassed on him.

Boy_with_a_Job: We can't just do nothing! Why did he cut you?

Wonder_Teen: He said I was his.

Boy_with_a_Job: What's it like, just random stabs or what?

Wonder_Teen: It's on the side of my wrist. I'll show you.

*Img_008_00001

Boy_with_a_Job: Fucking hell, that's horrible! What's that inside the box, a J?

Wonder_Teen: Yeah.

Boy_with_a_Job: His initial?

Wonder_Teen: Yeah.

Boy_with_a_Job: He can't even draw a square around it properly, it's all wonky.

Tosser. Tell me who he is. I swear, I'll beat him up for you.

Wonder_Teen: No! Don't! Forget I said anything. I just needed to tell someone.

She'd already given him her real name the week before, and where she went to school. He'd told her he was called Neil. She was the only girl he hadn't bribed for money, nor had he persuaded her to send nude images. Even for him that was a bit mean, considering what she'd been through.

The next day, he'd gone to the school, showing the headmistress his fake ID and explaining that he was doing talks in the area about gang crime and did she have any in her school?

"Of course not," she'd said, indignant, although she'd looked shifty, guilty, as though she'd never admit to having a gang in her midst because it would reflect badly on her and be mentioned in an OFSTED report.

So he'd watched after school from his car, every day for a week, but he hadn't caught sight of Natasha to know who she was leaving with. At least if there had been a boy on the scene, he'd have known who he had to shit up.

And all along, it had been Joe fucking Osbourne.

Flint finished the first half of his sandwich and picked up the second.

BOY_WITH_A_JOB: HOW ARE YOU TODAY?

WONDER_TEEN: OKAY. MY WRIST HAS GONE ALL SCABBY. THE CUTS AREN'T DEEP, SO MAYBE IT WON'T SCAR. I'VE HAD A JUMPER ON ALL WEEK SO MY MUM DOESN'T SPOT IT. IF MY DAD DOES, HE'S GOING TO GO APE.

BOY_WITH_A_JOB: WHAT'S THE BOYFRIEND BEEN LIKE WITH YOU?

WONDER_TEEN: HE WANTS US TO HAVE SEX, BUT I DON'T WANT TO.

BOY_WITH_A_JOB: [ANGRY FACE] THEN DON'T. MAKE SURE YOU'RE NOT ALONE WITH HIM.

WONDER_TEEN: YEAH, I'VE TOLD HIM I'M GROUNDED AFTER SCHOOL, BUT HE SAID TO SNEAK OUT, SAID IF I DIDN'T HE'D CUT MY…HE USED THE WORD CUNT.

BOY_WITH_A_JOB: WHAT THE HELL'S WRONG WITH HIM?

WONDER_TEEN: I DON'T KNOW. I THINK HE'S FUCKED IN THE HEAD.

BOY_WITH_A_JOB: YOU REALLY NEED TO TELL SOMEONE. IF YOU DON'T WANT IT TO BE YOUR parents, go and speak to another adult you trust. A teacher, an aunt or uncle.

He'd realised, as soon as he'd hit send, that he'd gone into police mode, giving her advice in grown-up words.

Wonder_Teen: Who, though? Any adult would make me tell the police, then my parents will find out.

Boy_with_a_Job: Is that such a bad thing? He's already committed assault with a deadly weapon and threatening with menace.

Wonder_Teen: You sound like a cop yourself!

Boy_with_a_Job: As if. I just watch a lot of telly, that's all. I've been trying to think of a way for you to get rid of him.

Wonder_Teen: Maybe it's time for me to move schools. Mum hates mine, she never wanted me to go there, all the yobs do, but my mates from primary were going, so…you know how it is. If I switch to yours, you'll protect me, won't you? [laughing emoji]

He remembered how dread had sluiced through him, him working out how he could stop her doing that without blowing his cover—because he didn't fucking *go* to school—yet at the same time, despite his pervy penchants, he wanted to protect her from a different kind of predator. This girl had got to him somehow. She was no longer an object for him to exploit but a child in need of help.

Maybe there was some good inside him after all.

WONDER_TEEN: ARE YOU STILL THERE?

BOY_WITH_A_JOB: YEAH. SORRY, I WAS JUST THINKING. WHAT ABOUT SPREADING RUMOURS ABOUT HIM? OR THE GANG?

WONDER_TEEN: WHAT GOOD WOULD THAT DO?

BOY_WITH_A_JOB: I DON'T KNOW. [SAD FACE]

WONDER_TEEN: HANG ON A SEC. I'M GOING TO SPEAK TO MY MUM.

He'd switched to browsing, looking for his next target. He'd found joining in the big group forum chats, getting involved that way, tended to work better for luring girls to private message him. He'd relegated Natasha to the friend zone the minute she'd shown him that picture of what her boyfriend had done.

A discussion had caught his eye because of the amount of traction it had gained, the comments in the thousands, prompted by the question: *If you could do any job in the world, what would it be?* He'd saved it to favourites to revisit later.

WONDER_TEEN: OKAY, SHE'S WELL CHUFFED I WANT TO CHANGE SCHOOLS. I TOLD HER I WAS BEING BULLIED. GUESS WHERE I'M GOING?

BOY_WITH_A_JOB: [LAUGHING EMOJI] MY SCHOOL?

WONDER_TEEN: NOPE. SHE'S ONLY GONE AND SUGGESTED LONGFORD ACADEMY!

BOY_WITH_A_JOB: THE BOARDING SCHOOL?

WONDER_TEEN: YEAH, BUT YOU DON'T HAVE TO BOARD, AND SHE CAN'T AFFORD FOR ME TO DO THAT ANYWAY, BUT IT MEANS I'LL HAVE TO GET THE TRAIN TO SCHOOL AND BACK, AND SHE'S ALSO GETTING ME A NEW SIM FOR MY PHONE SO THE 'BULLIES' CAN'T MESSAGE ME.

BOY_WITH_A_JOB: DIDN'T SHE WANT TO SEE THE SO-CALLED MESSAGES?

WONDER_TEEN: I TOLD HER I'D DELETED THEM. [WINK]

Flint drank his coffee. She was twenty-two now and still popped on London Teens every so often, likely keeping up to date with the friends she'd made on there, although he'd managed to drift away from her years ago without it being too obvious he was cutting ties.

He checked whether she had a green dot beside her name in the members list. There it was.

He opened up a chat box.

BOY_WITH_A_JOB: BOO! REMEMBER ME?

WONDER_TEEN: OMG! OF COURSE I BLOODY DO! HOW ARE YOU?

BOY_WITH_A_JOB: I FOUND HIM. THE ONE WHO CUT YOU. JOE OSBOURNE, RIGHT?

WONDER_TEEN: OH GOD...

BOY_WITH_A_JOB: I KILLED HIM TODAY.

WONDER_TEEN: WHAT? [SHOCKED EMOJI]

BOY_WITH_A_JOB: I TOLD YOU I WAS GOING TO FIND HIM, AND I DID. YOU CAN SLEEP BETTER NOW. [LOVE HEART] OVER AND OUT.

He closed the chat box, then deleted it and the username. He sat back, pleased with himself for doing the right thing for once. The only worry he had was whether Janine would get curious and poke into this at the station, see if he'd ever gone to a school to root out a gang. But she'd said the less shit she had to deal with the better.

He hoped she stuck to that, otherwise he might have to get nasty.

His phone bleeped, and he panicked that it might be her—they'd swapped numbers before he'd left the warehouse. He checked the mobile, but there were no new messages. Could it be his burner, the one he used for his unofficial informants? He had a look.

GALAXY: HAVE YOU SEEN JOE?

Fuck. Fuuuuuuuuuuuuck!

Flint gripped the sides of his hair, tugging hard until his eyes watered. What the hell had happened to his life? Why had it gone so wrong? If it wasn't for Janine wanting to swan off, none of this would be happening. He hadn't expected Joe's disappearance to be noticed so quickly.

But of course it would be, you stupid bastard. He runs the fucking line and hasn't been answering his messages.

Where was Joe's phone? In his trackie bottoms pocket? Flint had spied money poking out of one of them, that's why Joe had been in Hailey's loft, but he hadn't seen any of the others taking anything else out.

What the hell was he supposed to say to Galaxy? He didn't need him on his back. He was also one of Flint's little grasses right from when he'd been a runner, but Flint had never bribed him, keeping him as a 'normal' informant. When Galaxy had moved up the ranks, Flint had said he'd help manage Joe and the runners if they'd be grasses, too. They'd come to a mutual agreement. Flint had never told Galaxy that he had the others under his thumb, and they'd never told their boss just what a tosser Flint was to them. He'd scared them too much by saying he'd tell Galaxy they were skimming drugs off him, and money.

Now, with Joe out of the picture, he was better off distancing himself from the line since the twins knew it existed. He couldn't afford for any of them to tell The Brothers what he'd been doing, despite him saying it had been done with his police boss's blessing. It meant the line had to relocate, away from Cardigan. If he got it shut down, there'd be nothing to find.

FLINT: NO IDEA, MATE. GLAD YOU GOT HOLD OF ME. THERE'S BEEN A DEVELOPMENT. GET YOUR SHIT OUT OF THE LOCK-UP, AND I MEAN *NOW*. DON'T GO TO THE TRAP HOUSE AGAIN — WHATEVER'S IN THERE, LEAVE IT. TAKE YOUR BUSINESS OFF CARDIGAN.

GALAXY: WHY, ARE YOUR LOT RAIDING IT?

FLINT: NO, WORSE. WORD ON THE STREET IS THE BROTHERS HAVE GOT WIND OF IT.

GALAXY: SHIT!

FLINT: LIE LOW. DON'T CONTACT ME. WE'RE BETTER OFF SEVERING OUR CONNECTION SO THEY DON'T SEE US TOGETHER. GOD KNOWS HOW MANY spies they've got on the streets. I don't want you getting in the shit for being a grass to me instead of them. We don't know each other, we never met, okay?

Galaxy: Got it. Laters. And thanks.

Flint sighed out his anxiety. Galaxy wouldn't want anyone knowing he spoke to a copper on the regular, it would ruin his street cred, so Flint's secret was safe. The last thing he needed was the twins finding out he was involved in the line and it had nothing to do with work. He'd miss the bribe money, though, *and* fucking with the kids for fun.

Maybe it was for the best. He had other people to fuck with now, money to be made off the twins. Twists of fate happened for a reason, and he'd just roll with the punches, because rowing against the Wilkes' tide was a feat he'd never conquer, so he wouldn't bother trying.

His oars weren't strong enough.

Chapter Twenty-Seven

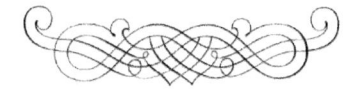

Pete Osbourne lived in Blanchard Crescent which consisted of a square-ended horseshoe of homes built in the fifties with a communal green in the middle, although it was more mud than anything where kids probably played football on it. George, in his Ruffian disguise, sat beside Greg in his ZZ Top getup, their little white van nice and toasty, obscure in the darkness of the evening. Today's side logo advertised PANELS R US, and in black suits and gold ties, they were ready to enter number five to convince Pete he'd make a fortune by selling generated energy to their company.

A bearded Ichabod, with a bowler hat and peacoat on, perhaps so any neighbour focused on his outfit rather than anything else about him, sat in a stolen car parked ahead, collected courtesy of their thief, Dwayne. Ichabod would be their lookout, because they planned to kill Pete in his own home. This was so poor Mrs Osbourne could collect any life insurance as there would be a body, plus she would be free to marry anyone else should she wish to try her luck with another fella.

Mason had discovered where the Osbournes lived, and Ichabod had been here since an hour after they'd left the warehouse, reporting that he'd overheard a conversation between Mrs Osbourne and her neighbour at seven p.m. over their adjoining front garden fence. He'd given the twins a warning—the neighbour had only come out when she'd heard the front door shut, so she was possibly a nosy beak and they might want to watch themselves.

The chat had revealed Pete's wife had a date with the doctor at the evening surgery in Bethnal Green and wouldn't be back until ten, what with the amount of busses she had to get on, owing to the fact Pete didn't want to give her a lift because *he* had a date with a six-pack of lager and a family-sized bag of cheese Doritos. Whether or not he'd have the spicy salsa dip she'd bought to go with, Mrs Osbourne didn't know. Her neighbour apparently preferred onion-flavoured hummus but understood it was an acquired texture.

"Why can't you drive yourself?" Mrs Hummus had wanted to know.

"Because Pete doesn't want me driving at night on my own."

"More like he's outright said you can't. I've heard the rows through the wall, love, I know what goes on. You can't kid me."

The shit Ichabod must hear when he's on surveillance.

The clock clicked over to seven thirty-five, and George was done with waiting. No one had left their homes for twenty minutes, so he reckoned it was safe to get the deed done while everyone was engrossed in the TV. He left the car, checked around one more time, and waited for Greg on the pavement. Greg held a clipboard and pen, and they made their way up the garden path. George opted to ring the bell instead of knocking, hoping to remain undetected by Mrs Hummus.

A light flicked on behind the frosted glass. The door opened, and a fuck-off wide man with a baggy black T-shirt over his distended belly, grey trackies poking out of the bottom, glared at them, his salted brown hair sticking up every which way.

"Yeah?" That word exposed his teeth. One of them was missing.

"Good evening, sir," George said, Scottish accent.

"Don't call me sir. It winds me up."

George held back the need to hit him. "We're here from Panels R Us and—"

"Fuck off." Pete went to shut the door, his jowls wobbling.

"Do you not want to make money, then?"

Pete paused and peered through the small gap, then he widened it enough for them to see half his body. His eyes held a gleam. George wouldn't be surprised if pound signs popped up in them.

Pete's expression turned sly. "What do you mean, make money?"

George launched into his prepared spiel, although he worried about fucking it up because he hadn't practised it enough. "Our company provides solar panels, rented by the homeowner, which generate energy from daylight. We split the earnings from the sale of that energy to the bigger companies."

"You said *rent* the panels. That'll *cost* me money."

"It won't cost you a penny. The rent is deducted from your earnings. You won't notice the cash being taken out because you didn't have it in the first place."

Pete frowned. "I don't get it. So I'm basically paying you to rent panels, on *my* house, when it should be *you* paying me to rent my roof space. Without people's roofs, you'd have no business."

Yep, I fucked up. Didn't think of that. And that's why I'd never be a good salesman.

George scrabbled to save himself. "Of course, we *could* accommodate you on that as one of our top-tier customers if you're willing to have the *whole* of your roof covered, Mr..."

"Osbourne. How much are we talking? What would I get?" Pete opened the door wider and folded his flabby arms.

"An average of one thousand pounds."

"A month?"

George smiled. "A week."

Pete grinned and scratched his crotch. "You'd best come in, then."

He lumbered down the hallway and into the living room at the back, plonking himself down on an empty Doritos packet, a tub of salsa on the coffee table. He was three lagers down, the open cans tossed on the floor by his crusty bare feet.

George walked over to stand in front of him. "Can you turn the telly up, pal?"

Pete grabbed the remote. "Like this programme, do you?"

The volume rose enough to hide the pop of a gun.

George whipped his out and aimed. Fired, the bullet entering the man's forehead. He didn't stick around to gloat over the damage, they had to get out of there sharpish. In the kitchen, he left the prepared padded A4 envelope full of cash, which included a note warning the wife to keep the payment to herself. Typed on the front: MRS OSBOURNE – PRIVATE. There was enough for a funeral and for the woman to have a much-needed holiday after she got over the shock of her husband's murder and the fact her son hadn't come round for a visit. Hopefully, Joe would be suspected of killing his own father then legging it.

Must get Janine to go with that narrative.

George opened the front door and checked in with Ichabod who gave the thumbs-up for the all-clear. They left the property, in there barely three minutes, and then they were off, Greg driving, keeping to below the speed limit, Mad George's laughter filling the van.

Natasha lived with her boyfriend and baby son in an average area on the edge of Cardigan. Mason had discovered her whereabouts, and Will had sat outside in a car, keeping watch. On the way back from Pete's, Will's text had come through that the boyfriend had gone out with the crying baby in a vehicle, perhaps to get the child asleep, so Natasha was alone. George and Greg had to drive home to collect a wedge of cash, plus it had taken twenty minutes to get to the house, and as George didn't know how long her family would be out, he wanted to get this done and dusted. Greg had opted to stay in the van.

On the way to the front door, George signalled for Will to leave. Glad of his Ruffian disguise, he rang the bell, the large money envelope in a gloved hand. It contained twenty thousand, and he hoped she'd take it. If not, he'd drop it on her garden path and walk away, then she'd be forced to pick it up and accept it.

She opened the door, dishevelled, likely knackered because of the baby. She frowned at him. "Yes?"

"Joseph Osbourne won't be giving you any more trouble," George said, all Scottish. "He's dead."

She stared, blinking several times. "Neil?"

"Who the fuck's Neil?"

"Um…it doesn't matter. Just some boy I used to speak to. So you're not him?"

"No, I'm his mate," George lied and handed her the envelope. "It's for what you went through."

She took it and ripped open the flap, peering inside. She raised her head, tears brimming. "But…"

"You got carved, yes?"

"Yes…"

"Then that's yours." George walked back down the path and left the garden, sensing her gaze on his back. He got in the van.

"How did it go?" Greg asked.

"All right, but she thought I was someone called Neil."

"Who's that?"

"Someone she told about Joe. It doesn't matter, she's got the money and knows Joe's snuffed it, so job done." But George wanted to find out who this Neil was so he could thank him for being there for Natasha. If he didn't, it'd bug him. "I'll see if Flint can shine a light on it. Maybe the kid was spoken to when Flint went to the school."

Greg sighed. "I thought you just said it didn't matter."

"Seems it does."

"Why can't you just leave it?"

"Because I don't like loose ends. Shut your face and let me do my thing."

George prodded the screen.

GG: Who's Neil?

Flint: ???

GG: Been to see Natasha to give her compensation. She thought I was Neil.

Flint: Ah, that's a kid she knew. He's dead now.

GG: How do you know?

Flint: I attended the RTA he was involved in. His parents died in it, too. Natasha might not have known because it only happened a month ago.

George didn't bother responding. "Let's go home, bruv. I need some grub."

Greg tutted. "I'm not cooking at this time of night."

"We've got a kettle, haven't we? A couple of Pot Noodles will do me. We'll need to stop off at the Co-op and get some tiger bread, though."

Greg started the engine. "I'll nick some of that for ham and piccalilli sandwiches."

George shuddered. "Why the hell you eat that yellow shit is beyond me. Foul. Just fucking foul."

"Don't knock it until you try it."

"I'll be knocking something else in a minute, and it's your fucking head."

Greg laughed and drove away. "Love you, too."

George pondered for a moment. "I was thinking."

"Oh God…"

"Hear me out. Stacey said her brothers beat Joe up. They might be people we could have on our team."

"Maybe. Now turn your work head off, for fuck's sake."

George reached for a lemon sherbet out of the glove box, stuffed it in his mouth, and crunched. It was the only way to stop himself from talking.

Flint shook all over. That text from the twins had shit the life out of him. They'd been to see Natasha—what the fuck?—and even worse, she'd mentioned Neil. He'd have been fresh on her mind because he'd not long contacted her and confessed to killing Joe. He should have just left it. She wouldn't have thought of him when George and Greg went to see her, then.

It's all right. If they question her more, she'll just mention London Teens. I use a VPN, so even if they guess what went on, they won't know it's me.

But why *would* they guess? It wasn't the first thing to come into someone's head, was it, that he might be perving on young girls.

He was just being paranoid.

Still, a sense of unease crept through him, and annoyance.

Those Brothers were far too nosy for his liking.

What if they went back to Natasha to find out *how* she knew Neil?

Chapter Twenty-Eight

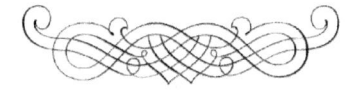

Hailey and Stacey met in Bumble's Café, both with wedges of cake and creamy coffees in front of them, cats with curled tails created out of powdered chocolate on top. Hailey hadn't intended to leave her house at all until Monday when she had to go to work, but Stacey had phoned, asking for a chat in person. Hailey supposed it was also because she wanted her half of the money before Chaz came home. Stacey planned to hide it in her She Shed, where she did her yoga and used the spray-tan machine Chaz had bought her. He never went in there, apparently, saying it was her private space.

He sounded like Riley. Perfect.

The suitcase containing Stacey's money stood beneath the table. They had almost six hundred thousand each, and Hailey had the irrational thought that other people knew what was in there, which was stupid. No one had X-ray vision. It must be her nerves talking.

"Did you sleep okay?" Stacey asked.

"Oddly, yes. I didn't expect to. Thought I'd be staring at the ceiling all night."

"I know what you mean. What's the first thing you'll buy?"

"A new sofa. Mine's on its last legs, although I won't be doing that until I've moved."

Stacey's face fell. "Oh. Where are you going?"

"Kent. Delaney's nan and grandad live there, so at least I'll know someone. I don't want to stay in that house after…well, you know. I thought it would be best to have a clean break. Wicked of me to say so, but I'll also have built-in babysitters."

Stacey nodded and cut a chunk of cake off. She speared it with a little fork. "I get it, but do you have to go all the way to Kent? We've only just become friends."

Hailey wasn't prepared to do anything she didn't want to anymore, nor would she let someone persuade her to do what *they* wanted. "Do you honestly want to talk about everything over and over? Because that's what we'll end up doing. Don't we both deserve to put it behind us now? I can't stand the thought of continually living in the past whenever we get together."

"True. We're bound to revert back to that because it's what we've got in common. You're right. I was being selfish. I'll just have to get my arse into gear and make new mates."

"Same."

"Bet you'll miss your mum."

"Yes, that goes without saying. She's been brilliant with Delaney, always there to pick up the slack, and it's about time she had a break. I was thinking about it this morning, and all she's ever done is look after me, and now her grandson. She needs a life of her own, and with me hanging around, she isn't going to get it. Do you know, she's never brought a man home since my dad walked out on her."

"Bless her. Have you told her yet?"

"No. I expect tears, but she'll see it makes sense in the end. Me and Delaney are holding her back."

"Will you get a job or live off you-know-what?"

"You-know-what for a bit. I'm frugal, so it'll last me bloody years. Maybe I'll do a uni course or something, try a different career."

"I admire your drive. After *him*, I had no oomph and ended up losing my job through depression, then Chaz came into the pub one night, swept me up, and made me a kept woman. Don't get me wrong, I love the lifestyle, but I'm *bored*."

Hailey shrugged. "Then get a job. What were you before Chaz?"

"A hairdresser."

"I saw an advert in the window of Under the Dryer the other day. Maybe try there?"

Stacey nodded. "I could do. With Chaz away a lot for work, I'm lonely." She eyed the case. "I could open up my own salon with that."

"And you'd explain the cash how?"

Stacey made an eek face. "Oh yeah. God, it's going to be so difficult, spending it in dribs and drabs."

"It's got to be done." Hailey tested whether her coffee was cool enough to drink. It was, so she had a few sips then tackled her chunk of Victoria sponge.

They chatted for a while, then Hailey had the urge to get outside and breathe the fresh air of freedom. On the path, she hugged Stacey, tears burning. They hadn't known each other for long, but it was surprising how close murder bound you to another person emotionally.

"Thank you, for everything," she said, pulling away.

"I'm so glad I met you." Stacey squeezed the tops of Hailey's arms. "Now go and smash it in Kent."

"And you smash whatever you're doing."

They parted ways, waving, and Hailey took the long way home, which took her past Blanchard Crescent. A police car was parked outside one of the houses, and a few neighbours stood gossiping on the edge of the muddy green. Two cordons had been put up, blocking a property off and the section of public footpath in front.

A woman appeared from the house closest to the edge of the crescent, her arms folded beneath her boobs. She must be about fifty, her hair in a shoulder-length bob Hailey quite fancied growing hers into.

"Terrible business," the lady called. "Did you hear what happened?"

Hailey went closer and met her at her garden gate. "No, what?"

"Pete Osbourne copped it."

Hailey's blood seemed to freeze. "Who's that? I don't know anyone who lives here."

"Ah, right. Well, you should have seen it down here last night. Blue lights flashing, a ruddy ambulance. Before all that, poor Amy came out of her house screaming, oh, must have been about tennish because the news was on. I got up to see what all the fuss was about, and she said Pete was dead—that's her husband. He'd been shot."

"That can be arranged. Actually, it will *be arranged."*

Hailey shivered and drew her coat fronts one over the other for extra warmth. Had George done this? Already? Had kicking Joe's dead body not been enough to appease his Hulk and he'd had to come here?

"Blimey," she said. "That's really awful."

"I saw him. Saw him dead. She asked me to go inside with her."

"Oh God, are you okay?"

"It creeped the life out of me to be honest. Sorry, I didn't introduce myself. I'm Belinda."

"I'm Cora."

"I used to know a Cora. A right spiteful muffin if ever there was one, but I'm sure you're not like that."

"Not if I can help it, no. So you saw the body, you said."

"Oh yes, and it was bleedin' awful. Most of his brain must have been on the curtains behind him—shame, because they were a nice set. Ruined now, of course. He was sitting on the sofa, a hole in his forehead, but I bet the back had been blown off. He was *staring*, worse than any staring I've seen off someone who's alive. I'll never forget it. It was like he could see right through me." Belinda shuddered. "Fucking bloke. I never did like him." She sucked in her bottom lip.

"Is his wife all right? I mean, she won't be all right, but…"

"She will be because life's bound to be much better without Pete."

"How do you mean?"

"He was right bastard. Knocked her about for years, and as for that son of hers... Nasty little fucker. And get this. Her son's not answering his phone, and the police have been round to his flat to see what's what, but no one's home."

"To see what's what?"

Belinda glanced over at the police car then back again. "We think Joe killed his dad. Makes sense, doesn't it? Pete gets his head blown open, and Joe's nowhere to be found? She's better off shot of them. Pair of fucking wasters. Do you fancy a cuppa? What am I like, keeping you out in the cold?"

Hailey was sorely tempted so she could get more gossip, but she didn't know whether Joe had ever shown his mother a photo of her. If she happened to come outside and spot her...

"I need to be getting back."

"I should go in, too, and check the spuds. I'm making a roast, enough for Amy to join me, and that lovely liaison officer she's got in there with her. Laura? Lara? I don't fucking know. Anyway, I've got a big enough chicken, so it'll stretch."

"Take care of yourself," Hailey said.

"You, too. Tarra now." Belinda turned to face the murder house, probably hoping someone from the green would trot over and chat to her.

Hailey pushed on, her mind whirring. She'd swapped numbers with the twins yesterday so brought up her message app.

HAILEY: JUST BEEN PAST BLANCHARD CRESCENT. SOME WOMAN TOLD ME JOE'S DAD'S DEAD. DID YOU KNOW?

GG: I KNOW MOST THINGS. GO AND ENJOY THE REST OF YOUR LIFE.

So that was that then, George had done it.

Hailey walked on, now wanting a roast dinner since Belinda had mentioned it. She took her phone out and texted Mum. She may as well tell her about the plan to move to Kent. Get it over and done with.

HAILEY: FANCY ME TREATING YOU TO A ROAST DOWN THE RED LION ALONG WITH A FEW GIN AND TONICS? DELANEY'S WITH KEN AND POLLY.

MUM: IS THE POPE CATHOLIC?

Hailey smiled. God, she was going to miss her so much, but she had to move on.

For both their sakes.

Chapter Twenty-Nine

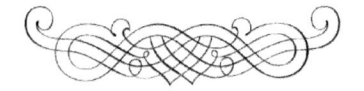

Stacey pushed the suitcase down her street and winced at the racket the wheels created on the pavement. The neighbours were curtain twitchers, and while they'd never introduced themselves to her, nor did they give her the time of day, she sensed their eyes on her every time she left or arrived at the house. The noise of the wheels was bound to have brought someone to their window. What if they mentioned it to Chaz, asking him if she was going away, seeing as the suitcase wasn't the same as the ones they used when they travelled abroad?

It was pretty new, so she'd get away with showing it to Chaz as if she'd bought it this weekend, plus all her makeup she'd store inside once she'd transferred the cash to her holdall. She had so much that it would be plausible for her to do that, like a vanity case.

She walked up their drive, then down the side of the house, through the gateway, and into the back garden. She fished her keys out of her handbag and unlocked the She Shed, more of a summerhouse, closing the curtains across the patio doors. Money transferred, she put towels on top of the bundles of cash and hid the holdall in the loft space beside her gym bag.

In the main area, she sat on her chaise longue and messaged George.

STACEY: GOT A QUESTION FOR YOU. CAN YOU MAKE MONEY APPEAR LEGIT?

Her phone rang, and she swiped to answer.

"I wondered when one of you would ask," George said. "How much?"

"Nearly six hundred K."

"We can arrange that. If you want something bought, we can do it and funnel the cash through the casino."

"I want a hair salon."

"What? You're setting up in direct competition with us?"

"No, it doesn't have to be in the East End, but I do need to be able to say I only run it and get paid a lot of money to do so."

"Why, because of your bloke?"

"Yes."

"Right. We can sort the deeds being put in your name, but there's the little problem of you registering your business with Companies House and risking your bloke seeing it on there. Why don't you let us own the salon, you manage it, then you can pay yourself 'wages' out of the cash as well as the wages we'll pay you?"

"Are you sure?"

"I wouldn't have suggested it otherwise. But there's a catch."

There usually is. "What's that?"

"It has to be called Curls and Tongs, and you'll need to store a few things in there for us. If they're ever discovered by the police, you know nothing about it."

"Done. Will there be a safe so I can put this cash in there?"

"Yep, one for you, one for the salon. I wanted to talk to you, actually. How are your brothers fixed for jobs?"

"Why?"

"Because if they're good at kicking the shit out of people, we might have some work for them."

"I'll send you their numbers."

"Cheers. Listen, we'll talk next week after we've secured a property. We're off to the Taj for a curry lunch. Oh, did Hailey get hold of you?"

"We met for cake and coffee not long ago, why?"

"So she hasn't mentioned about Joe's dad?"

"No…"

"He's dead. Tarra."

Stacey blinked at her phone, stunned. "Bloody hell, they work fast."

She lay back, dreaming of her new salon—and her new life, Joe-free. It was going to be all right at last. She'd give it a good go at putting this behind her, and maybe one day she'd be able to tell Chaz. But she'd worry about that later. For now, she had a business to plan.

Chapter Thirty

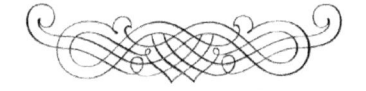

Janine had decided to get her chat session with Flint over and done with. On Monday morning, she sent her DS, Colin, off on a wild goose chase and met Flint in a freezing park. She'd wrapped up warm in her new coat that was more like a sleeping bag and sat at a wooden bench table hidden behind a massive pine tree. Flint appeared from behind it, giving Cameron, who lurked nearby, a bit of a glare.

"Don't look at him like that, he's my bodyguard."

"Fuck me, is that something you get when you work for the twins? I don't want any fucker following me around." He sat opposite.

"Why, got something to hide?"

"No!"

"To answer your question, a bodyguard is something you get from the twins when people in The Network might kill you, but that's almost over now. Only one left to catch last I heard. Oh, and he's my boyfriend, too."

"Right. So, what words of wisdom are you going to impart?"

She could see now how irritating she'd come across to George and Greg that first time she'd spoken to them. No wonder they'd got arsey—or more specifically, George. Flint was giving off the same vibe.

"Number one, cut the attitude. I was exactly like you when I started, and being a belligerent arsehole won't get you anywhere. George will hate you for it, your life will become a misery, and if you're not careful, you'll end up dead. I promise you, he won't think twice about putting you in the Thames."

"I can't help it. I've been forced into this so I'm a bit resentful. I've got my own little side earners going, I was doing fine on my own, then those two oafs show up with their PI and basically tell me what the rest of my life is going to be like."

"I get it, I do, but why bother fighting when you can't win? Why resist when you're only going to have to give in eventually? It took me ages to work out that I was better off obeying. All right, I still got arsey, but I learned not to moan about it so much. Think of the positives. The money—I'll miss that, I can tell you—and knowing that if anyone gets in your way, they'll go missing just like that. You'll be a prized asset, kept safe. George is the most evil, lovely person I've ever met, and I couldn't have anyone better in my corner than him and Greg—and Cameron, of course. Ichabod is also a good man, as are many Cardigan employees. You didn't do too badly on Saturday, so it can't all be bad."

He shrugged. "I did what I had to."

"You mentioned side earners. If whatever you're up to is something they'd hate, stop it, now, because if they find out, it's just not worth it."

"I've already canned a few revenue streams."

"A *few*?"

"Off-the-books informants. They pay me to keep them out of the nick, plus they give me tip-offs."

"Bloody hell. Are you after losing your police job or what? So what hustles have you kept?"

"I thought you said the less shit you know…"

"You're right, I'm better off oblivious. If you cock up, that's your problem and your consequences. Before I forget, when we're at the station, it's business as usual. If I start being your friend now, it'll look off. I'm barely anyone's friend. Let's go through some scenarios. We'll start with a basic request from the twins and how it works. Don't write anything I say down, keep it in your head. Ready?"

"Not really, but go on."

Janine smiled. She was going to enjoy watching him squirm.

Chapter Thirty-One

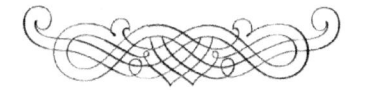

The doctor had upped Amy's anti-depressant medication. It would help, he'd said. He thought it was the early menopause causing her symptoms, her need to have an extra boost, but how could she tell him it was Pete and Joe who were the root of it? How could she say that for years, those two had abused her? She'd gone on the tablets originally based on the lie that she

was depressed. Opening up to a doctor, someone in authority, with the bald truth would have her either arrested or sent to the funny farm.

Normal people didn't plot their husband's deaths.

She got off the bus and walked up the crescent, weary but determined to plod on. Pete wasn't exactly in the best of health these days, and every New Year celebration, when she made her resolution, she hoped that this *year he'd die. She wasn't old, in her forties, and there was still a lot of fun to be had. She could afford to wait.*

She slid her key in the lock and stepped inside. The telly was on loud, and it grated on her nerves. Hadn't she thought, years ago, that Pete's hearing had been affected? At least there weren't sounds of moaning coming out of the speaker, so he hadn't put porn on while she'd been out. She couldn't face his verbal torment this evening, telling her she'd let herself go. But she'd been eating healthily for years and had lost weight, so whatever he said was a lie. While he *had put weight on so had no room to talk, not to mention that missing tooth. He wasn't exactly Brad Pitt, was he.*

She took her coat and shoes off, hung her bag up, put on her slippers. Same old shit, different day. At least the higher meds would have kicked in after a couple of weeks, so she'd feel a lot better, and anyway, her job gave her something to look forward to. She'd left the laundrette, like she'd told Mum she would, and worked as a helper in the care home Lil's mum used to live in before she'd died. She was going through training so she could get stuck in and look after the old folks properly.

She sniffed. Something smelled off. Maybe Pete had eaten the salsa after all.

In the kitchen, she went to reach for the kettle and frowned. A thick manilla envelope stared back at her, on the front: MRS OSBOURNE – PRIVATE. What the hell was that all about? Had someone posted it and Pete had left it for her? Unusual for him, he'd normally have opened it, didn't believe she should have any privacy. She reached out and picked it up, feeling the weight of it, then ripped open the tab. Inside, money, lots of it. She pulled it out, neat bundles held by elastic bands, plus a folded piece of paper. She read the typed words, her mouth hanging open.

There are times when people deserve happiness, and this is one of them. Before you ring the police, you need to hide the package and dispose of this note. In front of the coppers, act according to the scene in your living room. Oh, and you're welcome.

She read it again, trying to make sense of it. Why had someone given her money? Why would she need to ring the police? Was this something to do with Lil? What was in the living room? She didn't dare go there, yet she had to. But what about the money? She should get rid of it first.

Worrying her arse off over who'd given it to her and why, Amy shoved the cash back in the envelope and stuffed the note in with it. She opened the front door a little bit, ever mindful of the nosy neighbours, and peeked out. She had an idea, and it could just work as to why she was going out to the car.

Head inside the cupboard under the stairs, she rooted out the frost thingy for the windscreen, like a quilted blanket, hiding the envelope underneath it. Keys in hand, she marched to the car, opening the driver and passenger doors, bending to tuck the envelope under one of the seats. She got on with laying the windscreen protector in place, tucking it round the frame, then locked the car up.

Back inside, she closed the front door and stood in the hallway, sniffing again. It wasn't the salsa, she knew that with sudden certainty. It was blood, coppery and rich. Taking a deep breath to compose herself, she walked forward, taking her time to hold off the inevitable.

She entered the living room and stared.

Her beautiful curtains, stained with scarlet spatters and chunks of something meaty. An advert on the telly telling everyone to buy a pizza for ten quid. Empty cans of lager on the floor. The salsa pot on the coffee table. And Pete, a hole in his forehead, a dribble of blood down his face. It had already dried, so this must have happened a while ago.

She couldn't believe it. He was finally dead, and she'd had nothing to do with it.

It had to be Lil. She'd arranged this.

Amy shook all over. She was tempted to phone her but remembered she'd have to ring the police first otherwise it would look weird if they checked the log. Her phone was bound to be looked at to rule her out, and questions would be asked as to why she'd contacted a friend first. She turned and walked out, found her phone in her bag, shaking her head, trying to come to terms with what had happened. Pressed three nines and hoped to God she could pull this off, the shock, the grief, the every bloody thing associated with murder.

It seemed the dispatcher or whoever it was believed Amy was distraught, gently telling her to calm down, take a breath, go outside in case the intruder was still in the house.

"Do you want me to stay on the line?" the woman asked.

"No, I'll be okay, I'll be okay."

Then she rang Lil.

"What the fuck have you done?" Amy said.

"Good evening to you, too."

"Pete's dead."

"What?"

"Someone's shot him."

"Oh, fuck me sideways…"

"So it wasn't anything to do with you?"

"No! I'd have asked you first so we could make sure you were out."

"I was, thankfully."

"Jesus Christ, this is a turn-up for the books. Where are you?"

"At home, he was killed here. The police are on the way. But listen, I've got to be quick. There was an envelope on the side in the kitchen with money in it, a note." She quickly old Lil what it said.

"That sounds like The Brothers to me. They must have found something out if they've come and blasted Pete. That money will be compensation. Bloody hell…you've got to admit you're happy about it. You are, aren't you? Don't tell me you've had an attack of the guilts."

"I can't fucking believe it, that it's happened, but I'm over the moon yet scared shitless at the same time. I need to go. I'll speak to you later."

Time to act.

Amy rushed out of the house, screaming, "Help me! Someone help me! Oh God, oh God!"

Belinda was the first to come out, followed by her next door.

"What the fuck's happened?" Belinda stormed up the street, taking hold of Amy's upper arms. "Are you okay? What's he fucking gone and done now?"

"He's dead. Someone shot him in the head," Amy wailed loud enough for others to hear even with their doors closed.

Belinda glanced at her next door, then turned back and leaned forward to whisper in Amy's ear, "Was it you?"

"No! Where the hell would I get a gun from? I went to the doctor's, and when I got back... Christ... Come inside. Come and see."

Belinda trotted up Amy's garden path, on a mission, Amy following—she needed someone else to look at him, to confirm it really was over. Belinda's shriek of alarm and fear sent shivers through Amy.

I should be feeling like that.

"Oh my God, the way he's staring is shitting me up," Belinda said. *"Fucking hell, it's horrible."* She backed out of the room, bumping into Amy and screeching. *"Oh God, you scared me. I've got to get out of here. I've never seen something so nasty in my life."*

In the hallway, they clutched one another, Belinda clearly frightened, Amy giddy inside.

"Did you see anyone come?" Amy asked.

"No. But her next door might have. You know what she's like."

They went outside, their neighbour standing at her garden gate talking to a few women who'd also come out. Their husbands and some kids loitered on their doorsteps.

"Did anyone see anything?" Belinda asked. "Pete's been bloody well shot."

"Oh, bugger me," her next door said. "There was this van. One of those small white ones. It had Panels R Us on the side and something about solar energy. Two men got out, they had beards, and one held a clipboard. They were at your door. I was going to go round and have a word about the racket, the telly went right up, but I ended up falling asleep in the chair."

A police car, flashing lights turning the air blue, came into the crescent. Amy grabbed Belinda's hand, and the relief of it all, of finally being free, brought on a raft of tears. She choked on them, on the sobs, couldn't get any words out when the officers asked her questions. Belinda led her down the street to her house, Roger standing in the hallway, his face like thunder.

"Are you here again*?" he said to Amy and tutted.*

Both women sighed and said at the same time, "Oh, fuck off, Roger!"

The idea that Joe had killed Pete had been put to Amy by DI Janine Sheldon, the officer in charge of the murder squad team, a week after his death. They sat in Amy's living room on the patio chairs now her house had been released back to her, no longer a crime scene. The sofa Pete had died on was gone, as were the matching armchairs, every pair of curtains, the carpets, the kitchen lino, each scrap of furniture. Amy had arranged for the whole house to be emptied in her absence bar her personal things, which she'd packed into cardboard boxes and put in the shed. Her kitchen was being stripped out and replaced today, then painters were coming in a couple of days to go over the whole house, carpet fitters after that.

The life insurance had come in quicker than she'd expected, within days, all one hundred and fifty-seven grand of it, and she supposed, because the police had sent them an email confirming murder, that Life & Death didn't have a leg to stand on in disputing it. Mum had offered for her to kip round there, but Amy had been staying with Belinda, much to Roger's chagrin, and couldn't wait to have a brand-new interior, no memories attached to anything. As Roger had made it quite clear Amy's presence was getting on his wick this morning, she'd booked herself into a Premier Inn and would kip there until her house was complete.

DS Colin Broadley got up and stood where the old fire surround had been. The square hole would be bricked up, because she'd opted for one of those electric efforts that hung on the wall, white, long and sleek, stones inside with fake flames. She'd gone for modern stuff, the minimalist look, and Joe wasn't welcome to see any of it. She didn't have to have him in her life anymore, and she'd changed the locks to stop him coming in.

"We still can't find Joe," Janine said. "He hasn't contacted you?"

"No. I doubt he will. We don't get on. Me and Belinda—my neighbour—have already had this discussion. For him to disappear around the time his dad was killed… It's a bit suss. I thought they got on, but maybe they had a row."

"We've searched for Panels R Us, but the company doesn't exist. There's no trace of the van. Is that something Joe's likely to have done, gone to all that trouble to arrange for those men to kill his father?"

"He isn't the nicest of people, I have to say. I wouldn't put anything past him." It was good to get that out, to be able to say it with no guilt attached.

"During our investigation, we discovered your son ran a county line before he scarpered."

"What's that?"

"Drugs. Unfortunately, there's no proof in his flat that he's been doing that, just rumours. We got a warrant to search his home on account of him being a person of interest. We did, however, find a gun, but it isn't the same one used in Pete's murder. If Joe contacts you, you must let the police know, because if he has other weapons and is armed, things could get dangerous."

"Oh, I will. If he's done wrong then he has to pay for it."

"Good. Okay, that's about it for now. We've got your number, so if anything comes up, I'll give you a bell."

Amy stood and picked up her handbag. She'd left the spare key with her next door to let the men from the kitchen company in. Now she was going to see Mum before her shift at the care home.

Outside, she waved to Janine and Colin, getting in the car. As she drove away, she smiled at all this freedom she had, and it would be even better once Pete's body was released. She'd cremate him, going against his wishes.

One last fuck you.

Chapter Thirty-Two

Lil smiled at the twins walking into the laundrette. George had promised to come and tell her why those duvets had been washed despite being brand-new. It had bugged her ever since the night it had happened, and while he was days overdue, she'd keep her annoyance about that to herself.

"You're lucky you caught me here," she said. "I'm not singing at the care home today. They've got a magician in. Cuppa, I take it?"

She led the way into the staffroom.

"And biscuits if you've got any," George said. "I'm feeling a bit peckish."

"You're always bloody peckish," Greg grumbled.

"You're just jealous. It's not like I have a woman to watch my figure for, unlike you."

Lil switched the kettle on. "Relationship going well, is it?"

Greg smiled and sat at the table. "You could say that."

George took a perch. "He's loved-up to the bleedin' eyeballs. It's enough to make you sick." He slapped the table. "Right, the duvets."

He explained, and Lil felt so bad for Hailey and Stacey. Those poor cows, what they'd been through. It didn't bear thinking about, especially as Lil had suffered the same. Men and their nasty ways got right on her tits.

"The bloke they were going to kill was Joe Osbourne," George said.

Oh. Lil wasn't sure whether to pass that on to Amy or not. The woman was worried he'd gone to ground and would pop up again to hurt her. She was also convinced he'd shot Pete.

"So you dispatched Joe, then?" She spooned instant coffee into cups, not giving a fuck that George gave her a filthy look. "Listen, you, if you want that pod stuff, buy me a machine for when you drop by. Since when has instant not been good enough? You want to be careful else you'll turn into one of those posh bastards."

"Bore off." George yawned, although it sounded fake. "But yeah, Joe's dead. Let's not tell his mother, eh?"

"How come?"

"We need the narrative that he killed Pete."

"She already thinks that." Lil poured milk, added sugar, and took the cups to the table. Biscuit tin in hand, she passed it to George. "I take it you also did Pete. You did her a massive favour. She's been trying to kill him for years, and as for her not knowing about Joe, if you told her he's dead, she'd be relieved. He was a bastard to her, and she couldn't stand to look at him."

"How come you know that?"

"She worked here for years, remember."

"Oh, she's *that* Amy. Blimey. Got any other hidden gems we should know about?"

George gave her the side-eye, and she had the sneaky suspicion Ichabod had opened his mouth, revealing what she'd told him.

"I've got plenty, but they're secrets, which is why I'll be keeping them to myself." She'd change the subject, get it away from her. She didn't want them knowing her business if she could help it. "Amy said she received an envelope. I told her that sounded like something you'd do, that it'd be compensation. Have you been to see her to explain?"

"Nah, she can think what she likes. If she's happy Pete's dead and Joe's off the scene, you can leave it at that."

"Right, will do." She sipped her coffee. "I'm not surprised it was Joe who Hailey and Stacey were after. The shit he's done… The way he treated his mother is disgusting. Still, he's gone now, so like you said, we can leave it at that." In other words, as far as she was concerned, this was over and she'd never speak about it again.

"Cheers."

She tutted. "I know the rules."

They talked about Stacey opening a new hair salon and Hailey moving to Kent. Everything had been tied up in a nice neat bow, justice had been served, and although Amy hadn't been the one to pull the trigger, she'd finally got her revenge. Lil prayed the woman could put it all behind her now, but if she was anything like Lil, she'd carry it around with her forever.

The twins left, and she got straight on the blower to Ichabod. "What the fuck have you been saying to George and Greg?"

"What are ye talkin' about?"

"George asked me if I'm keeping any secrets from them."

"That's feck all tae do wid me. I said I'd keep it tae myself, and I have. Like I told ye, unless it impacts them and the Estate in the future, I'll never tell them."

Lil didn't detect a lie, but the man worked for the ruddy twins, so he'd be used to fibbing convincingly. "Right, well, sorry for accusing you, but I don't trust easily, you know that."

"Ye secret's safe wid me, I promise."

She ended the call and went back out the front. Three women and one man sat waiting for their laundry. One stared at the suds pressing against the glass door as if she had the weight of the world on her shoulders. Lil couldn't be arsed to go and ask her if she was all right. This Pete and

Joe business had been enough excitement for now. Two service washes were due to finish in half an hour, so she'd get on with the folding and packing, then stop for food. She had a nice cob roll—ham salad with Branston—and a jam doughnut for afters. In the meantime, she'd be a cow on social media.

Twenty minutes later, the door opened. Some bloke with a salt-and-pepper beard came in and went straight to a washing machine. His black beanie hat, pulled low over his eyebrows, didn't hide the colour of his hair which peeked out at the temples, grey and curly. He pushed his laundry into a machine, and she had the uncharitable thought that his donkey jacket could do with going in there an' all.

He approached the counter and took his wallet out. "Have you got any change for me to buy some washing powder?"

The sound of his voice sliced through her psyche, sending her blood cold. She knew it, had heard it in the dead of the night after sex, in the mornings, the afternoons. The beard had disguised him well, as had the wrinkles he'd acquired over the years since she'd last seen him, but now she stared into his eyes, the truth of it being him slapped her in the face, her heart thudding.

"Hello, Lil," he said.

She'd act unfazed. "The Guv'nor, as I live and breathe. How the devil *are* you?"

"Not bad, Lil, not bad."

"What brings you back to the Big Smoke?" She took the tenner he handed over and sorted the change, placing it on the counter so she didn't have to touch his hand when she put the coins in it.

"You, amongst other things. I've missed you something rotten."

A shiver wriggled up her spine. He was the one who'd got away, the one she couldn't kill because he'd fucking legged it before she'd had the chance.

But it seemed she had the chance now.

All good things come to those who wait.

She smiled. "Fancy a drink in the Red Lion later, then?"

Hopefully, it'll be the last pint you drink, shitface.

To be continued in *Razors,*
The Cardigan Estate 29

Printed in Great Britain
by Amazon